NEVER FORGIVE

(A May Moore Suspense Thriller—Book Five)

BLAKE PIERCE

Blake Pierce

Blake Pierce is the USA Today bestselling author of the RILEY PAGE mystery series, which includes seventeen books. Blake Pierce is also the author of the MACKENZIE WHITE mystery series, comprising fourteen books; of the AVERY BLACK mystery series, comprising six books; of the KERI LOCKE mystery series, comprising five books; of the MAKING OF RILEY PAIGE mystery series, comprising six books; of the KATE WISE mystery series, comprising seven books; of the CHLOE FINE psychological suspense mystery, comprising six books; of the JESSE HUNT psychological suspense thriller series, comprising twenty four books; of the AU PAIR psychological suspense thriller series, comprising three books; of the ZOE PRIME mystery series, comprising six books; of the ADELE SHARP mystery series, comprising sixteen books, of the EUROPEAN VOYAGE cozy mystery series, comprising four books; of the new LAURA FROST FBI suspense thriller, comprising nine books (and counting); of the new ELLA DARK FBI suspense thriller, comprising eleven books (and counting); of the A YEAR IN EUROPE cozy mystery series, comprising nine books, of the AVA GOLD mystery series, comprising six books (and counting); of the RACHEL GIFT mystery series, comprising eight books (and counting); of the VALERIE LAW mystery series, comprising nine books (and counting); of the PAIGE KING mystery series, comprising six books (and counting); of the MAY MOORE mystery series, comprising six books (and counting); and the CORA SHIELDS mystery series, comprising three books (and counting).

An avid reader and lifelong fan of the mystery and thriller genres, Blake loves to hear from you, so please feel free to visit www.blakepierceauthor.com to learn more and stay in touch.

HER LAST HOPE (Book #3)
HER LAST FEAR (Book #4)
HER LAST CHOICE (Book #5)
HER LAST BREATH (Book #6)
HER LAST MISTAKE (Book #7)
HER LAST DESIRE (Book #8)

AVA GOLD MYSTERY SERIES
CITY OF PREY (Book #1)
CITY OF FEAR (Book #2)
CITY OF BONES (Book #3)
CITY OF GHOSTS (Book #4)
CITY OF DEATH (Book #5)
CITY OF VICE (Book #6)

A YEAR IN EUROPE
A MURDER IN PARIS (Book #1)
DEATH IN FLORENCE (Book #2)
VENGEANCE IN VIENNA (Book #3)
A FATALITY IN SPAIN (Book #4)

ELLA DARK FBI SUSPENSE THRILLER
GIRL, ALONE (Book #1)
GIRL, TAKEN (Book #2)
GIRL, HUNTED (Book #3)
GIRL, SILENCED (Book #4)
GIRL, VANISHED (Book 5)
GIRL ERASED (Book #6)
GIRL, FORSAKEN (Book #7)
GIRL, TRAPPED (Book #8)
GIRL, EXPENDABLE (Book #9)
GIRL, ESCAPED (Book #10)
GIRL, HIS (Book #11)

LAURA FROST FBI SUSPENSE THRILLER
ALREADY GONE (Book #1)
ALREADY SEEN (Book #2)
ALREADY TRAPPED (Book #3)
ALREADY MISSING (Book #4)
ALREADY DEAD (Book #5)
ALREADY TAKEN (Book #6)

ALREADY CHOSEN (Book #7)
ALREADY LOST (Book #8)
ALREADY HIS (Book #9)

EUROPEAN VOYAGE COZY MYSTERY SERIES
MURDER (AND BAKLAVA) (Book #1)
DEATH (AND APPLE STRUDEL) (Book #2)
CRIME (AND LAGER) (Book #3)
MISFORTUNE (AND GOUDA) (Book #4)
CALAMITY (AND A DANISH) (Book #5)
MAYHEM (AND HERRING) (Book #6)

ADELE SHARP MYSTERY SERIES
LEFT TO DIE (Book #1)
LEFT TO RUN (Book #2)
LEFT TO HIDE (Book #3)
LEFT TO KILL (Book #4)
LEFT TO MURDER (Book #5)
LEFT TO ENVY (Book #6)
LEFT TO LAPSE (Book #7)
LEFT TO VANISH (Book #8)
LEFT TO HUNT (Book #9)
LEFT TO FEAR (Book #10)
LEFT TO PREY (Book #11)
LEFT TO LURE (Book #12)
LEFT TO CRAVE (Book #13)
LEFT TO LOATHE (Book #14)
LEFT TO HARM (Book #15)
LEFT TO RUIN (Book #16)

THE AU PAIR SERIES
ALMOST GONE (Book#1)
ALMOST LOST (Book #2)
ALMOST DEAD (Book #3)

ZOE PRIME MYSTERY SERIES
FACE OF DEATH (Book#1)
FACE OF MURDER (Book #2)
FACE OF FEAR (Book #3)
FACE OF MADNESS (Book #4)
FACE OF FURY (Book #5)

FACE OF DARKNESS (Book #6)

A JESSIE HUNT PSYCHOLOGICAL SUSPENSE SERIES
THE PERFECT WIFE (Book #1)
THE PERFECT BLOCK (Book #2)
THE PERFECT HOUSE (Book #3)
THE PERFECT SMILE (Book #4)
THE PERFECT LIE (Book #5)
THE PERFECT LOOK (Book #6)
THE PERFECT AFFAIR (Book #7)
THE PERFECT ALIBI (Book #8)
THE PERFECT NEIGHBOR (Book #9)
THE PERFECT DISGUISE (Book #10)
THE PERFECT SECRET (Book #11)
THE PERFECT FAÇADE (Book #12)
THE PERFECT IMPRESSION (Book #13)
THE PERFECT DECEIT (Book #14)
THE PERFECT MISTRESS (Book #15)
THE PERFECT IMAGE (Book #16)
THE PERFECT VEIL (Book #17)
THE PERFECT INDISCRETION (Book #18)
THE PERFECT RUMOR (Book #19)
THE PERFECT COUPLE (Book #20)
THE PERFECT MURDER (Book #21)
THE PERFECT HUSBAND (Book #22)
THE PERFECT SCANDAL (Book #23)
THE PERFECT MASK (Book #24)

CHLOE FINE PSYCHOLOGICAL SUSPENSE SERIES
NEXT DOOR (Book #1)
A NEIGHBOR'S LIE (Book #2)
CUL DE SAC (Book #3)
SILENT NEIGHBOR (Book #4)
HOMECOMING (Book #5)
TINTED WINDOWS (Book #6)

KATE WISE MYSTERY SERIES
IF SHE KNEW (Book #1)
IF SHE SAW (Book #2)
IF SHE RAN (Book #3)

IF SHE HID (Book #4)
IF SHE FLED (Book #5)
IF SHE FEARED (Book #6)
IF SHE HEARD (Book #7)

THE MAKING OF RILEY PAIGE SERIES
WATCHING (Book #1)
WAITING (Book #2)
LURING (Book #3)
TAKING (Book #4)
STALKING (Book #5)
KILLING (Book #6)

RILEY PAIGE MYSTERY SERIES
ONCE GONE (Book #1)
ONCE TAKEN (Book #2)
ONCE CRAVED (Book #3)
ONCE LURED (Book #4)
ONCE HUNTED (Book #5)
ONCE PINED (Book #6)
ONCE FORSAKEN (Book #7)
ONCE COLD (Book #8)
ONCE STALKED (Book #9)
ONCE LOST (Book #10)
ONCE BURIED (Book #11)
ONCE BOUND (Book #12)
ONCE TRAPPED (Book #13)
ONCE DORMANT (Book #14)
ONCE SHUNNED (Book #15)
ONCE MISSED (Book #16)
ONCE CHOSEN (Book #17)

MACKENZIE WHITE MYSTERY SERIES
BEFORE HE KILLS (Book #1)
BEFORE HE SEES (Book #2)
BEFORE HE COVETS (Book #3)
BEFORE HE TAKES (Book #4)
BEFORE HE NEEDS (Book #5)
BEFORE HE FEELS (Book #6)
BEFORE HE SINS (Book #7)
BEFORE HE HUNTS (Book #8)

BEFORE HE PREYS (Book #9)
BEFORE HE LONGS (Book #10)
BEFORE HE LAPSES (Book #11)
BEFORE HE ENVIES (Book #12)
BEFORE HE STALKS (Book #13)
BEFORE HE HARMS (Book #14)

AVERY BLACK MYSTERY SERIES
CAUSE TO KILL (Book #1)
CAUSE TO RUN (Book #2)
CAUSE TO HIDE (Book #3)
CAUSE TO FEAR (Book #4)
CAUSE TO SAVE (Book #5)
CAUSE TO DREAD (Book #6)

KERI LOCKE MYSTERY SERIES
A TRACE OF DEATH (Book #1)
A TRACE OF MURDER (Book #2)
A TRACE OF VICE (Book #3)
A TRACE OF CRIME (Book #4)
A TRACE OF HOPE (Book #5)

PROLOGUE

Ryan Harris waited in the woods, gripping his gun. He was ready for the takedown. Behind him, he heard the muttered voices of his team, and further away, the race of an engine as a cruiser sped along the road.

Finally, thanks to the hard work of the local police team in the small town of Sunnybrook, Minnesota, they had tracked down the source of the online threats that the department had been receiving in the past few days.

It seemed impossible that such violent and diabolical threats had originated from this humble wooden cabin, about two hundred yards into the forest. But clearly it was not impossible. Ryan could see the tall spire of a signal booster on the far side of the cabin's roof, and a couple of solar panels also. Whoever lived here was well connected, hooked up to the online world.

Police had discovered that the cabin was owned by a man named Marc Sudbury, but not much was known about him. He lived off the grid and had no close relatives or employers in the area. But Ryan had seen old ID photos of him. The man was tall, bearded, with an intelligent gleam in his eyes and, Ryan thought, a shifty-looking face. It was likely that Marc had sent these threats, but with so little information on him, it was also possible that someone else was using his cabin. The identity of the criminal would only be confirmed in the takedown.

Now, that was just a minute away. Ryan had a breathless feeling that time had telescoped, and was now concentrated into these next few intense moments.

The threats had first arrived three days ago from an anonymous and untraceable email address. Since then, the IT department had been working around the clock to isolate the source, and identify the IP address, which had been harder than it looked. At first, the criminal had used the dark web to send the emails, promising death, destruction, and annihilation to the local police, addressed to the deputy in charge.

"You are nothing more than criminals yourselves. You deserve to suffer and I will sabotage your vehicles to make sure you do."

1

"You and the team are going to end your days in fire; I will make sure of it."

"Shouldn't you be scared to set foot outside your police department? Because I'll be waiting, and I have you in my sights."

The IT department had tried a new tactic yesterday. They'd sent back taunting emails in reply, hoping to rile him and that in his anger, he would make a mistake. And Ryan felt amped that the tactic had worked. Yesterday afternoon, they'd sent an email at three-thirty p.m. He'd made a mistake, and had used the normal internet to send an angry and violent response to that email, instead of the dark web.

The reply had been sent at five p.m., which had given them the lead they needed in order to find where he had been at that time. The teams had been on it immediately, tracking the IP address. In the small hours of the morning they'd identified the cabin. And now, early in the morning, with the sun not even up yet, they had come back for the raid.

There was a light on in the cabin and he could see the flicker of a computer screen through the curtain, hearing music and voices. Clearly, the man who'd emailed them yesterday afternoon was awake and at home, confident in his anonymity.

"We're on the eastern border," the cops radioed from the car that had circled around to the far side of the forest, looking to block Sudbury if he exited that side.

"We're behind you and ready," the three cops behind him confirmed, breathlessly.

Not bad work, Ryan thought, for a team of small-town cops in Tamarack County, Minnesota. But it wasn't over yet.

It wouldn't be over until they had successfully entered the criminal's headquarters, which Ryan sized up as a strong, but weathered-looking building, approximately fifteen by twenty feet in size, with a wooden porch on the side facing the nearest tree.

A thin curl of smoke was issuing from the chimney, indicating that the criminal had built an old-fashioned fire for warmth, while using modern technology to deliver his threats. And so far, Ryan hoped, he had no idea that the team was surrounding his home base, ready for the raid.

That could change, and fast. They needed to get in there as soon as possible, before Sudbury realized they were there and prepared himself to meet them. Ryan had no doubt that he would be armed and dangerous. The element of surprise was critical.

The takedown would be the riskiest part of this so-far seamless operation. He needed to use speed and aggression.

"Go around the back," Ryan instructed two of the police following him.

He had realized Sudbury was clever and cunning. If he knew they were closing in, he could easily evade them, double back, slip away. Ryan wasn't going to let that happen. The back of the cabin needed to be guarded.

And then, he and his partner would have to get ready for the most dangerous maneuver they had yet attempted.

"We're going to storm the door. Be ready. Weapons drawn. The fugitive may be armed."

He looked at the cabin, which looked peaceful and innocent. A light inside, a fire in the hearth. He imagined the man seated at a wooden table, with a laptop open, issuing his threats. Would he be a fundamentalist, a doomsday scenario follower with an aptitude for IT? Ryan didn't know. As yet, his motives were unknown.

Even though he didn't think they had been seen, he kept his gun ready, moving forward as quickly as he could. He didn't want to be caught in the open if Sudbury had a gun and chose to fire upon them through a window.

Ryan felt glad of the Kevlar vest he wore; that would at least protect his center mass, the biggest target. And they were not going to hesitate. If he was armed, if he was holding a weapon, if he was even reaching for a weapon, then he would die.

"We're going in," he muttered to his team, glancing around, glad to see nods of agreement and that every officer looked as committed as he was to the takedown.

The plan was simple. He would charge the door and kick it in. He would rush into the cabin, followed by the three officers behind him. They would storm the interior and tackle Sudbury – or whoever was using his cabin – and take the man down before he had a chance to respond or fight back. They would arrest him, take him in, raid the cabin, and seize the device, or devices, he'd used to send the threats.

He looked around one last time. He had the support of all his team.

They were ready.

He was ready.

"Cover me," he said, and his team nodded.

He took a breath, and then took off, racing for the door of the cabin.

Feet drummed over the forest floor as the team behind him rushed toward the building, and around the sides of the cabin to the back.

Ryan leaped onto the flimsy porch.

"Police! Freeze!" he yelled at the top of his voice.

3

At the door, Ryan lunged, shoulder first, putting his full body weight behind the tackle. He hit the door with a gut-wrenching blow, bracing himself for the pain, and bursting through, into the cabin.

He blinked in the overhead light, breathing hard.

The cabin looked to be unoccupied. There was the desk, just as he had expected. On it was a laptop and a desk lamp, a notebook, and pens. But there was nobody sitting in the chair.

The voices and music were coming from a movie, playing on the laptop. Playing to nobody.

The bed on the far side of the room was unoccupied. The wooden door to the bathroom was open and the small toilet and shower could be clearly seen. There was nobody in there.

How could this man have disappeared, vanished into thin air? Was there a hidden bolt hole that he hadn't seen? Where had he gone? Ryan felt disconcerted and totally creeped out.

Behind him he heard the surprised murmurs of his team.

"He's gone!"

"He can't have disappeared?"

Feeling confused, and desperately worried that he'd evaded them, Ryan stepped forward.

A floorboard below creaked under his foot. He heard a strange, sizzling noise that lasted only a moment.

And then, there was a massive blast. A blaze of light brighter than he could imagine. A boom that exploded in his ears.

Ryan had the strange sensation of being thrown high in the air on a burning wave.

And then, nothing more.

The world evaporated into darkness.

CHAPTER ONE

Deputy May Moore sat at her kitchen table, scanning her laptop, scrutinizing the area maps and lists that she had set out on the screen. She was on the hunt, and determined to find what she needed.

"I'm not going to let you hide away," she whispered determinedly.

Even though it was a bright and sunny midsummer morning, the memory of the video that a stranger had loaded onto her laptop two weeks ago made her cozy cottage feel like a dark, uncomfortable, and unsafe place.

She couldn't believe that she'd received an actual warning to back off from the re-investigation of her sister's missing person case.

Someone had been waiting outside her parents' house in the small town of Fairshore, Minnesota, on the day when she'd had the terrible fight with her eighteen year old sister, Lauren. Someone had videoed the fight.

May was sure that person must have followed Lauren as she'd stormed off to the lake, and had taken her.

Now, this anonymous person had sent May the video, with a message to back off, to stop re-looking into the case, to stop trying to find out what had really happened ten years ago. Or they would take action.

May shivered as she thought about it.

Knowing that someone in this quiet neighborhood was following her movements, and knew she'd reopened the case, was scary. Terrifying, in fact. She had no idea who was watching her, who knew what she was up to, and who had actually broken into her house to leave this video on her laptop.

That was chilling. But May was fighting her fear. She was not going to give in to this cowardly warning. For a start, she'd bolstered her home security. Now, there were cameras outside the front door and side door, and also in the lounge and bedroom. Nobody was going to approach anonymously. Not anymore. She had a new security gate at the entrance to her bedroom, which she locked at night, so she wouldn't wake with a stranger standing over her bed.

And she was doing her best to work out who this person was. Who had lived in the area ten years ago? Who had been within sight of her parents' house? Who would have been able to stand nearby and watch, without causing suspicion? Who had the neighbors been?

There had been some movement in town. Some homes had been rented by tenants, who'd gone on to live elsewhere within Fairshore, or moved out of the area completely. Some families had split up, some had retired.

But May was sure she was looking for someone who had lived in or near the town then, and who still lived in or near the town now.

Keep your enemies closer. That was a saying she had always felt was very meaningful, and it resonated with her now. Perhaps that was what this person had done, figuring that she was the enemy, and might one day go looking for answers. Who knew if someone had been watching her for years? She felt unsure of everything right now.

May rubbed her eyes, pushing back a lock of her tawny blonde hair, fastening it under the hair grip again. No matter how difficult it was, she was going to narrow down the field of people who had the means and the motive to do this.

Because, if she did, then surely it meant there was actually a chance that Lauren could be found?

Disappeared without a trace did not necessarily mean dead. May had always wondered and worried why they'd never found her sister's body, despite a massive search and so much time passing. That fact had gnawed at her.

But as she checked her watch, she realized her search would have to wait for now.

Obsessed as she was with knowing the truth, and finding the source of these threats, she could not let it interfere with her duties. And, as the new county deputy for a couple of months now, May tried to set an example by being the first of her team to get to work every day.

It was seven-twenty-five a.m., and time for her to leave. The drive from the rural outskirts of Fairshore, where she lived, to the police department, took just five minutes. It was a small town.

She closed her laptop and packed it away. She checked that the back door of the house was locked and that all the windows were closed. It was deeply disturbing to her to feel a thrill of fear that someone might break into her house while she was out, and leave another warning message - or worse.

May didn't want to think about what the worse might be. But she had to be brave. She had to take the stance that by threatening her, this person was showing that they existed, and that they were threatened by her. That was the truth of it, and what she had to focus on.

They were real. And she was getting closer. They were the one who should be afraid now, not her.

As she left, locking the front door carefully behind her, May heard her phone start ringing.

She rummaged in her purse and pulled it out, her pulse quickening as she saw it was Sheriff Jack, her boss, on the line. A call from him before working hours usually meant an emergency, and May picked it up fast.

"Morning, Sheriff Jack?"

"May. We have a serious situation here."

She could hear it was serious. Jack sounded as stern as he ever did. She could imagine her gray-haired boss would be frowning, the lines that were etched on his face looking suddenly deeper.

"What's the situation?" she asked anxiously.

"Police in Sunnybrook tracked down a series of threats that were made against them. They got an email in return to one of their messages yesterday afternoon, which allowed them to pinpoint the IP address."

"Yes, I heard about those threats." May had seen the notification that the raid would occur. She'd had it on her to-do list today to contact Sunnybrook and ask if it had been successful, as well as congratulate them on tracking down the IP address.

Jack continued in a heavy voice. "They traced them to a cabin in the woods outside town. But when they went in early this morning to do the raid, the whole thing blew up."

May hissed in her breath.

"Was anyone hurt?" she asked.

Jack sighed. "Yes. Two good and experienced officers were killed instantly. Another three are in the hospital with concussions, broken bones, lacerations, and burns."

"No!" May's eyes widened. Cops killed? She couldn't remember the last time this had happened in Tamarack County. The loss of a police officer was an absolute tragedy. And an emergency.

"Where is the scene?" she asked, pulling herself together after the blow of shock had dissipated.

"It's a way off the main road, about three miles from Sunnybrook town center. I'll send you the coordinates now."

May watched her phone, waiting for the message. "Received," she said.

"The cabin is still locked down, and being searched by the bomb squad. It's not going to be easy to investigate, and there is most likely going to be no evidence available at the site of the blast. But I'm sending you out there now. As county deputy, you need to be on the scene and help manage the situation."

"Understood," she said.

"They're waiting on the bomb disposal team to arrive, and then they'll go in there. The FBI is also on their way; they've been called out, and are helicoptering in urgently."

May guessed, with a twist of her stomach, that would mean her older sister Kerry was en route to the crime scene. Kerry, the super-successful one of the family, who'd aced the FBI entrance exams when May had been overcome with nerves and flunked out. She was sure that the FBI would deploy Kerry to the scene, knowing she was originally from the area.

But this was no time to worry about family tensions. Not at such a terrible moment. May knew that she needed to do whatever she could to help out. This was a crisis. A state-level emergency, in fact, most likely a national emergency, playing out in their usually quiet county.

Jack knew she was prepared to give everything to the job, and that she was up to the task. He knew that she had what it took. He always had faith in her, and May always felt motivated to prove that he was right to do so.

"I understand," she said. "I'll be there."

May's heart hammered in her chest. It felt like she was being thrown into the deep end, into the very deep end. The investigation of a cop killer. A bomb blast.

She didn't know how she felt about that. Her head was spinning, and it was only seven-thirty in the morning.

"I'm not sure what's going to happen next, but I'll let you know," Jack told her. "For now, just get to the scene. We need as many people as we can on site. It's still a developing situation."

May had the feeling that this was going to be a day that she would remember for a long time.

"I'll be there in thirty minutes. I'll report in then," she said.

She still felt as if she was resonating with shock. Wired to explode? That was the most terrible, cowardly thing she'd ever heard of. Who could set something like that up and then flee, knowing people would be killed?

And how had the killer gotten away?

There were so many questions, and she needed answers. It was time to drive to the woods outside Sunnybrook, and see what awaited her.

May ended the call, and took a huge, deep breath to calm herself. Then she started her car, and headed out, as quickly as she could, to the scene of the crime.

CHAPTER TWO

May had never seen so many police on site at a crime scene. The ordinarily peaceful, small town of Sunnybrook was buzzing with frantic activity. As she approached the wooded area beyond town, she saw the road had been barricaded off to allow a hovering helicopter to land. Cars were parked in the emergency lane. Three policemen were redirecting traffic, and she saw two ambulances still on site, as well as an armored bomb disposal vehicle and two fire trucks.

She showed her badge when she pulled up, and the cops moved the barricade and waved her through.

Already, May was realizing that this was by far the biggest disaster in her entire career.

There was still smoke billowing into the air from a point in the woods, and May felt a frisson of dread as she saw the inky black, curling residue of the explosion, still dissipating into the clean blue sky. She imagined the violence of the blast. How terrifying it must have been.

She pulled up behind a Sheriff's Department car, which was parked just outside the barricade, and which had its light bar flashing. She squeezed between the police cars and vans and parked her own car next to the road.

May got out, feeling as if her stomach were still in her throat. She felt as if her whole world had changed, and as if she had just been catapulted into a new, and darker, reality.

Sheriff Jack was already on the scene, standing by the trail leading into the forest, and he was talking to the bomb squad leader.

May put her hat on, and went over to them.

"May." Jack acknowledged her with a nod. "The bomb disposal team is on site, and the FBI has just arrived." He indicated the helicopter. "It's a bomb site, but it's also a crime scene. Until we know what's going on in there, it's too risky to go further. We're waiting to make sure the area is cleared."

"What about the perpetrator?" May asked. "Have you identified him? Was he killed in the explosion?"

"We haven't been able to tell," the bomb squad leader replied. "We'll know more in the next half-hour."

"The bomb blast was designed to kill and maim. It's a miracle that the cops who surrounded the back of the cabin are still alive. They are reporting that just before the blast, the team leader shouted that the cabin was empty. If the perpetrator set this up and then fled, it looks as if we've got one hell of a case on our hands," Jack emphasized.

"Who were the cops that were killed?" May asked, dreading to know. It was likely that she'd met them personally, or else had heard of them.

"Ryan Harris was the team leader, partnered with Lester Biggs," Jack told her in a quiet voice.

May nodded solemnly. They were both younger than her, and she'd been present at a parade where they had received awards from the local mayor for their conduct in a case. They were good, up and coming cops who had a promising career ahead, until the killer had ended it.

She felt a flare of resolve that although nothing could bring them back, they could at least get justice by capturing the killer.

At that moment, May saw Kerry disembarking from the helicopter.

Her sister's slim figure was unmistakable as she jumped down, landing lithely on the tarmac and staring around her, taking in the activity, staring at the crime scene tape cordoning off the trail head, while running a hand through her short, blonde hair.

Behind her, her investigation partner Adams climbed out, looking stern and focused.

Three other grim-faced FBI agents that May didn't know followed them down.

Kerry hadn't seen her yet, May noticed. She was turning back to the other agents, deep in conversation.

May knew this meant the local cops would have to wait on their decisions. Being a disaster of statewide magnitude, where cops had been killed, the FBI would be handling the case from this moment on.

She walked over to the crime scene tape at the trail head, hoping that with all the combined might of these different investigation departments, this killer could be found. She wished there was something she could do, some action she could take. Even though she knew the scene was still unsafe, she wished she could go down and help with the search for evidence.

But there was nothing she could do to hurry the process along. For now, the only thing she could do was stand by until she was given instructions by the new team in charge.

It was easier for May to see the crime scene from here. There was a path that led down into a small valley, with trees and bushes lining it, but the cabin itself was visible.

She caught her breath at the scale of destruction. The ground itself was blackened. The cabin was nothing more than one flame-streaked wall. Everything else had been annihilated. Nearby trees and bushes were still ablaze, and she could see fountains of water as the fire department fought to control the fire.

Paramedics in protective jumpsuits were loading body bags onto stretchers, and May swallowed hard as she witnessed that sight.

Then, from behind, a hand clapped her in between her shoulder blades and she let out a cry of surprise, spinning around to find herself staring into Kerry's intense blue eyes.

May suspected she saw a flash of amusement there at her involuntary startle. But then Kerry was back to her serious, professional, on the job persona.

"May. Good to see you here."

"Hey, Kerry," May said.

Kerry turned to the other FBI agents. "This is my sister, May Moore. She's the county deputy, and will be working with us on this case. May, meet the rest of the team. Adams you know. My other colleagues are Special Agent Ted Billings and Special Agent Robert Chris, and Senior Special Agent Keith Ross is also on the scene for now, just to manage the initial steps of our investigation."

"Pleased to meet you," May shook hands with them. They were very similar to Adams. Definitely the same stamp of individual. Billings and Chris were both in their late twenties or early thirties, both with close-cropped dark hair and focused, determined expressions. Keith Ross looked to be in his forties, with a shaven head and piercing, ice-blue eyes.

The group of them stood in silence for a moment, looking down at the scene of devastation.

"The area is still not declared safe," May said, remembering Jack's warning. "It'll be another half-hour or so still."

"That's okay," Kerry said. "We had a glance down as we flew over when arriving. It's unlikely there will be any useful trace evidence that investigators can pick up, after a bomb blast of that magnitude."

"Exactly," Ross added. "It'll be up to the bomb squad to analyze the type and origin of the explosives used, which will hopefully be helpful to us. So we'll have to wait on their findings."

"Hopefully, we'll get results soon," Ted Billings emphasized.

12

"That's not where we need to focus now," Kerry told her.

"Where do we need to focus?" May asked.

"We're dealing with a very dangerous serial killer," Kerry said. "Perhaps one of the most dangerous we've ever seen. He's escalating, and he's also becoming increasingly bold, brazen, and ruthless. He's a cold-blooded murderer, who will keep killing and killing, until we find him. If we are going to stop this guy, we need to move fast, and work as a team."

"Agreed," Adams said firmly.

"Who is the killer?" May asked, feeling concerned. Had he detonated this type of explosive blast before?

If that was the case, then most probably he had not died at the scene and was still at large, and perhaps even in her area of jurisdiction.

The thought gave her chills, but she knew that was what it took to be county deputy. Terrifying as it was to have a killer like this at large, she was going to do whatever it took to catch him.

But first, she needed to learn more about the background.

"We'll explain all that to you. Let's get started with the briefing. I suggest we go to the Sunnybrook police department. We can use the briefing room down there, and I'll explain more about who he is and what he's done so far" Kerry decided. "We'll ride with you."

CHAPTER THREE

As May walked back to her car, she was worrying deeply about the case. A killer who had used explosives before - and now this person was at large, perhaps still in Tamarack County?

With a shiver of dread, she wondered how they were going to track him down, without incurring terrible risk to all the police involved. She couldn't handle the thought of one of her own team falling prey to an explosive-wired trap.

Then, listening to the tramp of boots behind her as the group followed her up the slope to the road, May's worry veered to a more practical subject.

How were she and five FBI agents all going to fit inside her car? Apart from Kerry, they were all big guys.

May was fretting over whether she should do two trips, or whether it might be better to call a cab or an Uber, if any were around in this small town.

But luckily, that predicament was resolved as she was relieved to see a familiar vehicle pull up, with a squeal of brakes.

Owen Lovell, her deputy and investigation partner, had just arrived. He climbed out of his car, looking horrified. Never had she seen such an intensely serious expression on her tall, good looking investigation partner's face. His brown eyes were wide. His hat sat askew on his neatly trimmed dark hair.

At last, she had some moral support, and felt a flicker of reassurance in this scary and unexpected scenario.

"May!" he said. "I came here as fast as I could. I was in the swimming pool at gym when Sheriff Jack called. This is terrible." In a lower voice, he added, "I see the FBI are here."

"I'm glad you're here, Owen," May said, the words heartfelt. "We're going straight to the police department in Sunnybrook for a briefing on the situation. Would you mind giving Special Agents Billings and Chris a ride?"

"Sure, of course," Owen agreed, giving the two a firm handshake. "Morning, gents. Good to have you here. Terrible situation."

May hustled over to her own car. Kerry climbed in next to her, and Adams and Ross got in the back.

May set off on the short drive into town, which led past the local church on the corner, and some shops and restaurants in the compact town center. Beyond them, on the far side of the local coffee shop, was the police department. May wasn't surprised to see that it, too, was a hive of activity this morning.

The parking lot behind the building was almost full. May took the last space, and behind her, Owen parked on the sidewalk outside.

As they hustled to the police department, there was a strong smell of good coffee coming from the lobby. May guessed that the coffee shop next door was working overtime to supply enough caffeine for all the personnel crammed into the building.

She followed the scent inside, where she saw a deputy at the front desk she recognized.

"Morning, Ella," she greeted the short, brown-haired woman who usually had a ready smile but looked stressed today.

"Morning, May," Ella replied.

"Is there a meeting room we can use? The FBI is here and we have to be briefed," May said.

Ella looked alarmed. She got on the phone and spoke quickly.

A few moments later, she put the phone down and nodded.

"You can go through. The small boardroom is available. The team inside has just wrapped up. Second door on the right. Do y'all want coffee?"

"Yes, please," May said gratefully.

They all filed through to the boardroom. May could feel the tension thrumming in the corridors. Phones were shrilling. Tense voices were raised. Footsteps thudded in and out of the offices.

They all crammed into the meeting room, which had six seats around a round table, a whiteboard, and a small desk in the front of the room. It had a nice view over the local park, May saw, but at this hour the green space was occupied only by a lone jogger and a woman walking her dog.

They all took a seat. Owen sat to Kerry's right. To her left was the big boss, Keith Ross. He sat down, drumming his fingers on the table thoughtfully as Kerry opened her laptop and prepared.

May looked around, at all the serious, professional faces. This was her first meeting with a high-level FBI team, she realized. And as deputy, she was representing her county, and would need to live up to their standards and expectations.

"Okay, folks, let's get started," Kerry said. "I'm going to brief you about the current situation regarding the killer, and what we know so far."

May listened intently, getting her notepad out of her purse in case she needed to write anything down.

"As yet, his identity is unknown to us," Kerry said.

"Unknown?" May asked, surprised. She'd thought the Sunnybrook team had known who the criminal was that they were chasing down.

Kerry silenced her with a look that said, louder than words, 'I'm getting to that.'

May flushed red, subsiding in her chair as Kerry continued.

"He has killed three previous victims, using the same technique - a bomb blast. So we are referring to this unsub as the Bomber. The Bomber has killed a female lawyer, a restaurant manager, and a schoolteacher. The cases only recently came to our attention, as the crimes have been committed in different counties and a couple of them were first thought to be accidental explosions. So until a few days ago, nobody realized it was a serial killer at work."

May's eyebrows shot up. Three kills, apart from today's explosion? All innocent people, pillars of society too. How had he managed that? And why them?

There was a tap on the door, and Ella brought in a tray of coffees. She placed it quickly on the table and left. Everyone focused on the coffees as Kerry continued. "The kills have taken place over the past few weeks. His technique changes, but it is always carried out by means of explosives. One of the more deplorable methods he used, with the lawyer, was that he captured and held her in an unused warehouse for a couple of days. During that time, he actually wired her phone up to the bomb, to be detonated when a certain number called in. Her husband tried to call her a few times over the days, but the phone was off. Once the killer had linked it, her husband's next call connected, and actually triggered the explosion."

May felt even more shocked as she heard this.

"Any links among the victims?" she asked.

"Not that we have ascertained," Kerry told her.

"What about the cabin in the woods? Who did that belong to then?" Owen asked.

"It belongs to Marc Sudbury, a man who moved off the grid a few years ago, and uses it as a base for taking YouTube videos of birds and mice, for cats to watch, believe it or not. That is how he makes his money. Through the advertising royalties."

"Cats?" Adams asked in surprise.

"Yes, cats," Kerry confirmed. "It was well set up with solar panels and wi-fi inside, which is probably why the bomber used it as the location to lure the police there. Therefore, police rushed to the cabin looking to capture the criminal, and walked straight into his trap," Kerry said, her voice solemn.

"So Sudbury was not there at the time?" Owen asked.

"He's on vacation in Florida. We've just been in contact with him and he had no idea this was even happening. He was horrified to hear it. Since the threats were undoubtedly sent from the premises, we surmise that the intention of the killer seems to have been, in this case, to lure police to the place and then detonate the bomb."

May shook her head. This evil was indescribable.

"And we know nothing more about him?"

"Only that he has been operating within Minnesota State, but this is the first time he has struck in Tamarack County. We're going to do everything we can to catch him before he strikes again."

"If he knew the cabin was there, and so well equipped, he must know the area quite well, or else have researched it thoroughly and recently," May suggested.

She saw nods all around the table at that observation.

May felt a chill run down her spine. The thought that the killer was familiar with Tamarack County, and could be anywhere in this area, perhaps planning his next attack, was very disconcerting.

"Of course, we are doing everything we can to catch him, and to protect all citizens in the area," Kerry finished.

"Well, obviously one good place to start will be to look into that email address, and see if we can find any links to it," Ross decided. "At some stage, the killer would have had to provide some information to set it up. It's just a case of how fast we can obtain it, and if it's still valid."

"Agreed," Kerry said. "I think we should set up base in this meeting room and connect with head office IT, and try to find more details on that."

"Billings and Chris, when the scene has been declared safe, you two are probably our biggest disaster scene experts," Ross then said. "I would suggest you two head back there and see what trace evidence can be found. Perhaps he left something behind while setting up the bombs."

"Will do," Chris snapped out.

That left May and Owen. She stared inquiringly at Kerry and then Ross, wondering what role she would be given, if any.

Clearly, Kerry didn't want to give her anything that the FBI could do better, and Ross didn't seem to be taking her or Owen into account at all. But May decided to come forward with a suggestion.

"Shall we take another look at the previous cases?" she suggested. "Perhaps there's more information to be gained from them now that we know the bigger picture, since the FBI has only gotten involved now? We could re-interview the lawyer's husband, for a start."

Kerry nodded. "That's a good idea. You could start with that case, and then look at the others. See what the local police reported, and then you go out and add to it. Perhaps you'll find a new piece of the puzzle," she suggested, in a way that told May she didn't think she would, and that ultimately the FBI, in consultation with their techs, would be the one to solve this.

"I'll get head office to send you the details on the recent case, involving the bombing of a criminal lawyer, Sheila Craig," Adams confirmed.

As she got up from the meeting table and headed out with Owen, May felt determined. This might be a small role, but she felt certain it would lead somewhere.

Three victims before this recent blast. Perhaps there was a link. And if there was, May promised herself she would find it.

CHAPTER FOUR

May couldn't help feeling relieved as she and Owen left the building and headed for her car. Being in the FBI meeting, and around a high-powered top management executive of the FBI, had kept her on the edge of her nerves, convinced she would say or do the wrong thing.

And this was no small matter. This was a massive disaster, something that had now attracted the attention of the FBI across the country.

And she, May, was playing a small part in solving it. Well, hopefully.

"I hope we can get results," Owen said as they drove out. May felt glad he was thinking along the same lines as her. As they so often did.

Things between them felt more relaxed now than they had a few weeks ago.

When Owen had asked her if they could date - and in his nervousness, hadn't gotten the message out in a way she could properly understand - it had been one of the most mortifying experiences of May's life.

For a while she had considered the possibility of accepting his offer and going on a date. And there were many advantages to it. Owen was cute, he was smart, he was great company.

But they were work colleagues. Doing that would change the landscape between them, and it would complicate things in a way she wasn't sure would be good. And it was a small town. In a small town, there was nowhere to hide. If things went wrong, it would be disastrous at worst, awkward at best. It might ruin what they had, and she valued that easy friendship more than almost anything.

So she'd decided against it.

She'd told Owen her decision, and he'd taken it well. She thought he was also relieved, in a way. He'd also agreed - it's a small town, and that makes things complicated.

Briefly, her thoughts flitted back to that threatening message she'd received.

Someone in this small town knew what she was up to. Someone wanted to stop her from pursuing Lauren's case. But who?

"Where are we headed?" May asked, getting her mind back to work again.

Quickly, Owen opened his laptop and scrolled through the information that had just come through, sent from a very imposing and highly secure FBI email address.

"We're driving outside Tamarack County. It will probably take us another half-hour," Owen said. "We're heading in the direction of a town called Springfield. That's where Sheila lived with her husband, Gary Craig. So he's the man we're going to see."

"He must be devastated," May said.

Owen nodded somberly. "It happened just a week ago. So I'm sure he must feel like it's the end of the world."

May couldn't imagine what it must have felt like for him when such a shocking thing had happened, and to know that he'd dialed the number that killed her? That was soul destroying.

She was not looking forward to the interview, but she hoped that the days that had elapsed since the bomb blast might, at least, have allowed Gary Craig to remember some details that had escaped his mind at the time.

*

Half an hour later, May and Owen arrived outside the large, gracious home a few miles from the center of the wealthy and prosperous town of Springfield. It was in a countryside setting, with a golf club down the road and an equestrian club opposite.

The house was large, with a gray pitched roof and a circular driveway with a fountain in the center.

May was feeling terrible about having to do this, and as if it would be opening old wounds. She'd had a lot of time to think about it on the drive. This would be a man who was grieving and distraught. He was likely to be a mess, and would not be interested in reliving the night of his wife's murder.

May sighed. This was not going to be easy, but she needed to keep a positive attitude and look for any small details that might help. As she'd thought previously, sometimes those things were only remembered down the line, after such a traumatic event.

She and Owen stepped out of the car and approached the grand front door.

May rang the bell, and waited. In a few moments, the door was answered by a housemaid wearing a smart blue and white uniform.

"Can I help you?" she asked, giving them a worried glance.

"Is Mr. Craig here?" May asked. "We're from the sheriff's office, following up on the case."

The housemaid nodded, looking distraught.

"He's here. He's in his study."

She led them through the hall, up a grand staircase, and into a library, furnished with polished dark wooden shelves, containing sets of antique books.

Mr. Craig was sitting at a large desk at the other end of the room. He looked up as they entered.

He was an imposing, dark haired man who looked as if he would dominate a boardroom table. Now, though, his hair was tousled and his face looked exhausted. From the glazed expression in his eyes, May felt absolutely sure that he was still on strong medication to calm him after the terrible guilt of knowing his call had activated the bomb blast.

"Mr. Craig, I'm so sorry about your wife," May said. "We're following up to try and gather more information. There's been another crime this morning."

His eyebrows raised. "Another crime? How long is it taking you to solve this?"

May nodded sympathetically. She couldn't say anything in her defense. Even though his voice was slightly slurred, she could tell he was seriously angry and letting her know it.

"We're doing everything we can," she replied. "We've just received the go-ahead from the FBI to ask you some questions. We've been brought in as additional help."

"And it's taken this long to get the FBI involved?" Mr. Craig demanded. "Now you're here? This is all so confusing, and why are there no results yet? Why should I even speak to you?"

"I realize it's difficult to have someone in your house that you don't know, who wants to ask you questions and bring up unpleasant memories," May said. "So feel free to tell me if you need space. We can step outside for a while or even come back later."

He nodded, and she thought her calm question had placated his anger slightly. "Okay. Carry on."

May sat down in one of the leather chairs facing him and Owen did likewise.

She already knew the timeline, knew when Sheila had disappeared, and what had played out. That was in the case summary that they had been sent. She didn't want to ask those questions again and make this grieving husband replay the days of worry after she'd disappeared on

21

her way to work, and the moment when he'd called her and her phone had rung once and then cut off. She knew that information already. She was hoping for other details.

"Sheila was a criminal lawyer, correct?" she asked, leading into the angle she wanted to explore.

He nodded. "She was. We are both lawyers. I'm a tax lawyer. It's how we met. We always knew her job was riskier than mine, but I never, ever thought this would happen."

"Did she have any controversial cases at the time?" May asked.

"She was defending a woman accused of theft, and a man involved in a tax evasion case. We looked into both of them with the police and we couldn't find anyone with a motive for doing this," he said heavily.

"And before that?" Owen questioned.

He made a face. "Look, she took on difficult cases, but she tried to steer away from murder in the past couple of years, now that she's more senior. She personally was not comfortable with that. She had to handle those cases eight years ago, when she had just joined the firm and was an up and coming criminal lawyer. Now she could choose, and she chose the more complex cases that were not as violent. White collar crimes."

"And anything personal in her life? Any problems, conflicts, unusual situations?" May asked.

Again, he shook his head. "Nothing like that. That's what was so weird about this. It was all so normal until it wasn't."

"How long have you been married?"

"Ten years. And we hardly fought." He sighed deeply. "We had a happy marriage. She was a happy person. She had literally no enemies, and that's in spite of her career."

"Did she receive any threats as a result of her work?" May was thinking of the anonymous threats that had led the police into this morning's trap. Maybe the killer made a habit of sending them. But Gary shook his head.

"No, not that I know of. She never told me about any threats and I don't think she received any. We didn't discuss work that much. Work was work, and to be left at the office. We both agreed on that. There were many other things to talk about."

"Thank you so much. I think we've taken enough of your time," she said, not wanting to intrude on his grief any further.

They got up and left quietly.

On the way down, May told Owen what she thought the next step should be.

"The bombing site where Sheila was killed is nearby here, in the town of Springfield itself. The coordinates for where she was held are in the case file. So we can actually go there and have a look. Perhaps something on the site will give us a lead."

CHAPTER FIVE

There was so much power in what the Bomber did. He felt as if he was unleashing the forces of nature, in retribution, to correct the balance of an unfair world.

The Bomber knew he was skilled, beyond the average. He knew his topic thoroughly. He knew his materials.

He knew the risk.

As he drove, he smiled, glancing down at his phone's small screen, and watching the video that played there. The last blast had been perfect. It had been a classic, textbook detonation. He knew because he'd stayed close enough to hear it and to see the plume of smoke, black and deadly, billowing from the destroyed cabin. He'd waited until he saw the police approach before hiding in the woods, but the camera had been in place, faithfully recording every moment until it got destroyed by the blast.

He'd known the police would arrive after he'd leaked the IP address in response to their emails, pretending to make a mistake, rather than sending from the dark web.

They'd taken longer than he expected to locate the cabin, but it had been worth the wait. Yes, it had been risky hiding in the trees, but the risk had been worth the joy of seeing a perfectly executed project come to fruition.

Immaculate planning, and a result that was everything it needed to be.

"Plan, prepare, execute," he murmured to himself. That was what he was living by.

In the cold days he'd spent in the past, with only his books and learning for company, his mind had turned inward. He'd been obsessed by the idea of revenge.

That had become his mantra.

"And I did it," he muttered. "I'm doing it, and I will complete it. Every step of the way."

He let out a gleeful laugh. He'd succeeded so far, beyond his wildest dreams.

"You're living the life you wanted to. Living your best life, achieving your goals," he told himself, glancing in the mirror, noticing a glimpse of his face, a face he had been told was handsome, if a little cold.

He'd succeeded. And the footage was here to prove it.

He glanced down at the screen, watching it again, rejoicing in the moment where the colors turned from brown and green, to white hot and then, a fade to black.

The camera had transmitted perfectly. He had already forecasted the right time of day and night when the video would capture the most action. The perfect picture.

He glanced down at the screen, at the video, again.

He knew he could not be caught. He was too careful, too skilled. Additionally, he'd taken too many steps to ensure his success. And now, he was going to relive this again and again.

Noticing that he had veered a few inches out of his lane, the Bomber hurriedly corrected himself. He did not want to draw attention to himself in any way. Even on these quiet, country, back roads that he knew well, his driving must be cautious and controlled. He should give police no reason to stop him.

He dusted his hands, then set them back on the wheel, being careful that in his elation he did not start to speed. He knew he needed to be invisible, apart from when he was not.

If only there was someone with whom he could share his pride and his achievements. But there was not, not yet. For now, until his project was complete, it was his own secret, to be told to nobody. Once it was all done, he would break the news to the person who needed to know.

If it was ever completed. He was liking it so much that he didn't want to stop.

This had not been an impulsive decision, to embark on this journey. This adventure.

He had worked on it for a long time, meticulously and carefully, researching the topic and gathering the right materials, calculating what would work and what would not work. He had been thorough.

Finally, he had made his selection. And then he had worked and worked on it, until it was time.

The world would see that justice had been served. It had not been served in the courtroom; it would be served by him, the ultimate judge and jury.

He had not rushed into this but had taken his time, studying and learning, knowing what he needed to do, exactly how he needed to do it. It had been a complex job because the research had to be done. The preparation undertaken. Materials had to be obtained, and he had done that carefully, taking time, so as not to cause any suspicion.

Locations had to be scouted out. Again, with care, because he wanted to stay a few steps ahead of the police. He doubted they would catch up, but it was unwise to be too confident. That would lead to disaster.

But he'd been worried at first. He was not normally familiar with being scared, but he'd felt fear before his first project. Was this really going to work? He'd been so nervous.

And no wonder, with so much at stake.

But it had been a success, and so had the next one. And now he was sure he could do it.

Now, in fact, he felt as if he was in the thick of it. And it was everything he could have hoped for, and more. He had footage of every blast, footage that delighted his eyes when he replayed it, because every moment seemed to accelerate the process of justice.

"Thank you, teacher dear," he muttered. He was grateful for his science classes. They'd taught him a lot. He'd liked his science teacher. With the right foundation, it had been easy to build on what he'd learned. IT and computer studies had been helpful, too. They had given him an excellent grasp of the technology he'd needed to set off these devices remotely.

Each one provided a unique and different surprise.

As he drove, he thought of his future, and what he would still have to do.

He would do the next one soon, that he knew. The timeline he'd set for himself dictated it, and so far, it was all going according to plan.

He had been meticulous in his planning. He had set one step in place after another, until he was certain that he could achieve his aims.

Unable to stop himself, he glanced down at the screen, at the video, again. The proof of his success was there, in that beautiful, unique footage of destruction.

The colors were swirling, as if in a gale, a whirlpool of colors that changed from green-brown, to white hot, and then to nothing. How he longed to view them in more detail later.

He had already decided that tonight, he would look at the video of the cabin that he had destroyed, and the targets he had killed. He would re-watch it, and revel in the knowledge that he had caused this destruction, and had the power to do whatever he wanted. He couldn't wait to take the next step, and to move on to his final targets.

The colors were still swirling in his mind, dancing like tiny flames, as he thought about what he'd done, and what he would do.

He knew this was bigger than others he'd read about and heard about who had embarked on similar crusades. He was deadlier than they were. He had power, and strength, and the clarity of mind to be able to execute his projects with precision and accuracy.

In comparison, they were small fry. He was a great man. And he would continue his work for as long as it took.

It was time to celebrate.

He reached over and grasped the bottle of vodka in the packet on the passenger seat. He was going to enjoy it. But later, not now.

It was his best life, and he was living it.

Laughing, the Bomber reached a stretch of road where there were no cameras. He knew that from his personal knowledge.

He put his foot down and allowed himself the luxury of speeding thirty miles over the limit.

After all, he had a destination in mind, and he couldn't wait to get there.

CHAPTER SIX

"So this is the crime scene?" May said, in shocked tones, as they pulled up outside the unused warehouse on the industrial side of Springfield.

She and Owen climbed out of the car, and approached the area, which was still taped off even though it had been fully searched a week ago.

May could see the scorch marks lashing up the walls, huge black streaks with areas of missing brickwork and gaps in the northern wall.

At one stage, she guessed that the warehouse had been locked with the same solid steel door that she could see on others across the road. Only this door was in tatters, the metal warped and buckled, with a huge hole blown in it.

May shivered as she approached, unable to stop her imagination from picturing what must have played out, and the violence of the blast. Her only consolation was that, undoubtedly, Sheila would have died instantly. But she must have been in terror for days beforehand. What kind of mindset did you have to possess to keep a woman trapped here, while setting up such a complex, evil way to murder her?

"This guy is sick, seriously twisted," Owen muttered, and May knew he was thinking along the same lines as she was.

"It's hard to think of anything worse, isn't it," she said.

"I guess there are no working cameras in the area," Owen said.

May shook her head. "No. I read the police report, and despite intensive research, they said they couldn't obtain any camera footage, and they had no idea what vehicle was used to bring her here. So that's a dead end unfortunately."

The area was so quiet it felt spooky. The only noise was the faraway sound of traffic crossing the highway bridge, and the closer rattle of sheet metal being disturbed by the afternoon breeze.

May paced around the outside of the warehouse, feeling her spine tingle at the sight of the scorch mark, and the hole in the door.

"I think he must have planned this whole scenario very carefully," she said. "This location was well chosen, and he would have paid the same attention to making sure that he didn't pass any cameras."

She stepped carefully under the tape and walked inside the warehouse, blinking in the sudden darkness. May held her breath, and tried hard to ignore the smell.

She took a look around, imagining what this prison might have been like for the criminal lawyer in her last days, hoping that by some chance there would be a shred of evidence that had not yet been picked up. But there didn't seem to be anything in this empty, desolate place to lead them any further.

The devastation was too complete to think that anything useful could be found.

On the side of the warehouse was a smaller, secure storeroom that the police determined was where Sheila had been held. May stared at the base of the walls where the scorch marks were particularly dark and vicious.

It was hard to imagine what it must have been like for Sheila, having to be imprisoned here. The room was tiny, a miniature prison within the larger warehouse, with a single window set high up in the wall, with a steel mesh covering it. The police report had stated that it had been previously used to store valuable electronic items that had to remain overnight within the warehouse. The killer must have done his research and known this room existed.

May was deeply disappointed not to find more, but she was not surprised. Forensics had already combed the area for clues, so what would be left?

She turned to look out at the warehouse yard, a rectangular lot that had been paved with rammed gravel. Big, concrete pillars had been installed, long ago, to support a walkway overhead. Metal girding, now rusted and discolored, and flaking, stretched across the roof.

Then she looked up, at the warped doorframe.

"There must have been a video camera attached there," she said, noticing the remains of a bracket on the wall, and three screw marks.

"Yes, they mentioned a ruined camera in the list of evidence. Unfortunately it was so damaged that they couldn't clearly identify which brand it was, or trace it back further. It was found on the far side of the warehouse. But you're right, it must have been mounted here to begin with," Owen said. "I doubt a camera like that would have survived in an unused warehouse without being stolen, so I guess that might mean that he put it up. Perhaps he was using it to monitor her and make sure she didn't escape?"

"Or perhaps he used it to film the explosion. If he was monitoring her, he could have removed it before he set the blast."

May shook her head, appalled by having to even voice such an idea. She cringed away from what it would take to do that. At least this told her more about this person, as much as she didn't want to explore his mind.

But she knew she had to.

He was someone who gloried in what he did, she decided. There was an element of pride, of satisfaction, in the fact that he was actually filming these scenes.

"He must be keeping the footage," she said. "And that will mean that if we can find him, he'll have evidence stashed somewhere. It's a sign of carelessness. The first sign we've seen, I guess. He's not covering his tracks completely if he's keeping a record."

"Our first sign of something we can use to get him," Owen said, sounding more encouraged. But May knew that there was still a long way to go.

"He's sneaky, sly, and clearly very knowledgeable. We're dealing with a smart killer here, a planner, with an evil mind."

Those were not very clear parameters but it was all they had so far.

"He's clever enough to pre-plan, and to cover his tracks. To be able to film the scene without being there, so that he can see the evidence of his own work."

It was terrifying to think that such an individual was at large in Tamarack County. And since he'd clearly been at work here, busy framing the most recent suspect and setting up the bomb blast scene in the cabin, May guessed he was still in the area. At least, she uneasily suspected he must be, and that they should assume he was.

She turned away from the scene, and looked around at the empty room. A place that had been Sheila's last home on Earth. And which sadly offered them no further clues.

Restlessly, she paced outside the warehouse, thinking furiously of what the next step could be. How did one catch up with such an elusive killer, someone who was not even on the scene when he murdered his victims?

"This is a dead end, I think."

"Agreed. There's nothing more to find here, apart from an insight into his mind, and that he's probably filming the explosions," Owen said. "That's worthwhile to know, but it doesn't get us further. What should we do now, May? The FBI is busy with the latest scene. I don't think we can be of help there."

"No, I don't think they need us. Combing a bomb site is too specialized, and so is tracking down an anonymous email address. But while we're driving back, let's look at the other case files and decide on our next step. Now that he's set off four bombs, that means four different cases to look back on. Maybe we can identify some common threads."

Owen nodded. "At least it's something we can do," he said disconsolately. May could tell he was discouraged by their lack of progress. So was she, but she was determined not to let the seemingly impossible circumstances get her down. Somewhere, there must be a chink in the killer's armor, a gap that would shed more light onto who he was.

"Let's drive back, and call Sheriff Jack on the way," May decided. "We've got an hour's drive and we might as well make it as productive as we can. If Jack can send us the details of the other cases, and you can have a look at it while I drive, we can decide if there are any loose ends, or any suspects in common, that we should be focusing on more closely."

CHAPTER SEVEN

As soon as they were in the car, May got on the phone to Sheriff Jack, hooking the phone up to hands-free as she powered onto the highway.

"We need your help, Jack," she said. "Now that there are four cases, there might be more common threads to be found that weren't obvious earlier on. We've already been to question the husband of the recent victim, Sheila Craig, and view the crime scene, but we'd like to work on the others as well."

"That's a good idea, May. Looking at all four with the perspective we have now, and especially the earlier three cases, might mean that you pick up something."

"Would you be able to send us the case files? We're driving back from Springfield, so we have some time on the road, and Owen can look through them."

"I'm going to obtain them for you, and send them to you straight away," Jack said. "May, whatever you can find, please go straight ahead and follow it up. There's no time to waste."

She could hear the urgency in his voice.

"Are you under pressure on your side?" she asked, guessing that he was.

"Yes. It's escalating, even with the FBI involved. We're being called on an hourly basis by the chief of police and the state governor, asking for progress updates. And because of the violence of these explosions, it is creating a media storm. Especially now that people are realizing that these bomb blasts in different parts of the state are all being carried out by one serial killer. That creates an immense amount of fear, as you know."

"Yes, I know," May said somberly.

"With the panic it's generating, any delay in getting answers is going to reflect badly on us."

May swallowed hard. She could sympathize with what Sheriff Jack must be having to handle.

"I hope we can get answers soon, and we'll go ahead as fast as we can."

"I'll email you the files in the next few minutes," Jack said.

May disconnected and glanced at Owen, who looked as worried as she felt.

"This is going to escalate in a bad way," he said.

"I hope we can find something - some common thread - in the other cases," May emphasized.

At that moment, Owen's phone and iPad began pinging.

"Here are the cases," he said, sounding more encouraged that at least now there was something to analyze.

"Take a look, and read the summaries out to me. Let's see what we have," May said, mentally crossing fingers that this would allow them to make progress.

They were driving out of town now, leaving the urban view behind, and the landscape was changing to the forested hills, lakes, and greenery that would provide a scenic backdrop for most of the way back to Tamarack County. She guessed the killer must have driven this same route, after murdering Sheila, with his next setup in mind.

She could only imagine how his mind had been buzzing with evil thoughts as he'd driven along the beautiful and scenic roads.

And now instead of being able to appreciate the view, May felt consumed with worry that they wouldn't find him, and that this would escalate into a national disaster, with the Tamarack County police departments at its epicenter.

Luckily, at that moment, Owen got the files into order and began reading.

"The first victim, killed a month ago, was a teacher at Woodbridge High School," Owen said.

May raised her eyebrows. That was just inside the borders of Tamarack County.

"I don't recall hearing about the crime," she said.

Owen shook his head. "It says here that the art teacher, Mrs. Flannery, age forty-seven, lived about fifty miles out of town on a farm with her son. So she resided outside of the county. She was murdered at her residence, not at school."

"That explains it," May said. "What happened?"

"She used to take her son's car to market every Wednesday, and it was wired to explode when she started it early on Wednesday morning."

"So the bomb was in the son's car?" May asked.

"That's correct. At first they thought maybe it was just a gas leak in the garage, or something that had happened with the fertilizer bags piled up there. It wasn't easy because the whole garage went up. It was only when the bomb squad got their results back a couple of days later, that they found it had been a deliberate bomb, planted in the car."

"And did they bring anyone in or have any suspects at all?" May asked.

"No, there were no suspects arrested. The police also didn't know whether the killer had actually meant to target her or her son, but everyone in the area knew that she went out and about in that vehicle on Wednesdays. So if someone had researched the crime, they would have known it would be her starting the car up that morning."

"That's interesting. Any likely suspects for either of them?"

"No. The son, Hilton, is a young farmer. He runs the place as a small organic farm and sells produce to the community. Mrs. Flannery was well liked at the school, it says here. She was divorced from her husband, but had been for years and he'd moved out of state. There were no problems with neighbors, no problems with staff on the farm; there are only three employees and they are all long term. The son wasn't at home that night; he was up north for three days, hauling cattle."

"So Hilton had an alibi?"

"Correct. It was investigated by the local police - not in our county - and they came up blank. The case is still open although now it has been linked to the others."

"Right," May said.

They had the background on the first case. What was the second?

"The second victim was in a restaurant that blew up. It was a roadhouse diner about ten miles to the west of Tamarack County. The victim was Barbara Vining, age thirty-three, who I think was the owner or manager of the roadhouse. They think that the bomb might have been activated when her sister called her. Mrs. Vining took the call late at night, as she was closing up. But it's not totally clear if it was linked to the call."

"I think I heard about that one," May agreed. "But not our county, so we were not involved."

"Exactly. It took place nearby but not within our jurisdiction. And she was the only victim."

May sighed. What could a restaurant manager possibly have done to deserve such a terrible fate?

"Did they narrow down the suspects?"

"She was divorced – her husband moved to Oklahoma a few years ago – and lived alone. They looked at a few suspects, based on recent visitors to the roadhouse. They interviewed a group of local boys who'd been in there the night before and caused trouble. But they all had alibis for later on. There was also an ex-waiter who they questioned in case he was involved, but they didn't take it further due to a lack of evidence connecting him with the crime."

Owen gasped.

"What?" May asked. The car swerved slightly.

"May, I've just made a connection here. Between these two cases. Something that obviously hasn't been picked up as yet. It can't have been."

"What? What have you found?" Now May felt seriously excited that this case might be moving forward. She couldn't wait to hear what connection Owen had made.

"The ex-waiter. He was a part-time waiter who worked weekends, but he was fired a couple of weeks ago. Now, he was also a student at Woodbridge High School. And he was recently suspended from the school."

Now it was May's turn to gasp.

This was a significant common thread between these two crimes, and she felt grateful that their re-reading of the case files had allowed them to pick it up.

A student at the school, had worked part-time at the restaurant. Both places had been the target of bombs, even though the teacher had been targeted, rather than the school itself.

And being fired and suspended was also significant. Any kind of trouble was always a red flag.

This student could be looking to take revenge on the people he perceived as having caused his troubles.

"What is the student's name?"

"His name is Cody Meyers," Owen said.

"And where does he live?"

"He lives a few miles from Woodbridge High. Perhaps we should go straight there?"

"I think so, definitely." May paused. "Does it say in the report why he was suspended from school? Or why he was fired?"

"I don't think they said why he was fired from the restaurant. I think it did include a written explanation from the school about the suspension. Let me find it."

Owen scrolled through the documents, and found the short paragraph.

"It just says he was suspended due to inappropriate behavior in science class. There's nothing more than that."

"I think we should drive straight to Cody's house. Let's question him, find out what it was, and why it got him suspended. Then we can also ask him what happened at work, and why he was fired."

Speaking to Cody would also allow them to check his alibi and whereabouts for some, or all, of the crimes. May wondered if Cody would be able to provide the necessary alibis, or if they might be on the way to the home of the killer.

CHAPTER EIGHT

Owen felt determined that if Cody Meyers was the common thread, they were going to get to him, question him, and make sure the case was watertight.

He glanced at May as she followed the route to the small ranch where Cody's parents lived – and where hopefully they would find him, too. He saw that May's face looked stern and worried.

He couldn't believe such a massive, violent case had landed in their jurisdiction. Seemingly out of the blue. Suddenly, Tamarack County was part of this killer's territory, and more than likely his current location. Suddenly, state attention and even national attention was focused on them.

Owen felt briefly intimidated by the sheer enormity of what they were up against. Even with the FBI involved, this was taking place on their local turf and as Sheriff Jack had pointed out, that meant they would be answerable and responsible.

It felt like a huge challenge for someone who had only joined the police two years ago and whose previous experience had been at an accounting firm.

But Owen reminded himself that he had joined the police because he wanted to make a difference. He felt compelled to try and help his community and his society fight exactly the kind of evil that this killer was displaying now.

Just like May was doing, he would approach this with all the courage and tenacity he possessed.

For a moment, thinking of May's character, Owen felt a flash of regret that she had said no to dating him.

He knew that he had to respect her wishes, but he couldn't help hoping that she might change her mind in the future, because his own feelings hadn't changed.

Every day that he worked with her increased his admiration for her competence and integrity, and his liking - okay, maybe it was more adoration - for her sense of humor and her insight.

As he looked at her now, he couldn't deny that he was still attracted to her.

Maybe her mind would change and he would get the opportunity he'd dreamed of, to take her on an actual date.

But he was a realist, and he knew that he couldn't force her to change her mind. He had to fully respect her own feelings and her own choices, especially as he knew she had suffered badly in the past with a nightmare divorce that had left her wary of getting involved again.

He owed it to her to give her space, and not to try and pressure her.

And in any case, Owen told himself firmly, this was not the time to worry about dating his investigation partner. Not when they were on such an important mission. He needed to push away these distracting thoughts, because they had a job to do.

They had to find the killer and stop him before anyone else died. That was the only thing that mattered now.

Finally, they were approaching the ranch, driving out into the countryside on a winding road that led through forested hills.

"Here we are," May said, slowing the car as they reached a rustic wooden gate with the number '14' on a pillar outside. The gate was open, and the driveway beyond led up the hill to the ranch.

"Looks like a decent-sized place," he said, admiring the neatly fenced fields, with knots of trees and well-kept outbuildings.

"It's a fair-sized spread," May agreed, accelerating up the drive and slowing as she reached the house. "Let's see who's home."

She pulled over and they both stepped out of the car.

The ranch was a long, red-roofed wooden building, with a white clapboard side. It was surrounded by a wide porch.

A few horses grazed in the field nearby, and Owen noticed a small creek flowed along the western edge of the property.

Owen glanced at May, feeling a flutter of nervousness in his stomach as they walked toward the ranch building.

They approached the porch, and May knocked on the door. There, they both waited, standing side by side. No one answered.

May knocked again, this time with a little more force. And Owen jumped as the door was flung open.

They came face to face with a tanned, blonde woman wearing a lavender cowboy shirt and jeans. Her expression was one of extreme annoyance.

"It takes me a while to get from the stables to the house! Don't keep banging on the door like that," she complained.

May stepped forward. "Deputies Moore and Lovell," she introduced politely. Owen always appreciated how she defused these situations. "I apologize for the repeated knocking. We're on a very tight schedule and would like to ask Cody some questions."

"Oh yes?" The woman gave a harsh laugh. "I doubt Cody will want to talk to you after the way you've treated him."

She glanced at Owen, then back at May. Owen blinked in confusion.

Still polite, May replied, "Ma'am, this is our first visit here. We haven't yet met Cody, but we do need to follow up on a recent case that he was connected with."

"He didn't do it," she said angrily.

"We're not saying he did," May said in a soothing voice. "We're just hoping we can ask him a few questions. Is he here?"

"My boy's had a hard time." The blonde raised her chin. "He was unfairly suspended from school because of inappropriate behavior in science class, and then he was interrogated by the police in a very unfriendly way, just for holding down a job that he was fired from! It was at least a week before that terrible explosion occurred."

"I'm sure that he definitely has his side of the story, and we'd like to hear it," May said soothingly.

Owen could see the woman's wrath beginning to evaporate.

"He's not in the house. He's in the cottage with a friend." She indicated a small building in the valley, a couple of hundred feet away. "That's where he lives. You can go there, but don't upset him. He doesn't deserve it."

"Thank you, ma'am," Owen said respectfully, feeling as if he should contribute in some small way to the dialogue.

She sighed heavily and shut the door in their faces.

Owen felt briefly worried that he just didn't have May's diplomatic touch. But May clearly wasn't worried. She was already turning in the direction of the cottage.

"I'm glad he's home," she said.

She began striding over the grassy hill, and Owen followed, wondering what would play out when they came face to face with Cody. He couldn't deny that he was curious to meet him, to see what kind of person he was, and if he could be involved in such terrible crimes. Already he got the impression that Cody was a loose cannon, and that his mother was protecting him from the consequences of his actions.

As they neared the cottage, Owen picked up the deep throb of heavy metal music, playing at full volume. The sound reverberated through the air, seeming almost to shake the wooden walls.

Smoke was rising from the cottage's chimney.

Owen frowned. It looked very thick and black to be fire smoke. What was going on inside there?

May was also looking perturbed.

"Perhaps we should take a look, and check it out, before we knock?" she muttered to him.

With explosive devices on his mind, Owen thought that was an excellent idea. If this man was their killer they couldn't be too careful, and needed to start taking precautions now. What if he'd wired a booby trap to activate when the door was opened?

May sidled around to the window. Then she and Owen peered through the rather dusty glass.

Owen's eyes widened as he saw the scene inside.

The cottage was set up like a science lab. There were containers of substances, test tubes, wires, and something that definitely did not look like a wood fire, smoldering in the grate.

Two men, wearing helmets and fireproof suits, were busy connecting the wires. They had their back to the window.

"Explosives!" May hissed.

Quickly, Owen took out his phone and snapped a few pictures, in case these were needed for evidence. His hands were trembling slightly, from the need to be as fast as possible, and also from the shock of stumbling on this nightmarish scenario.

He could not believe they had found the maker – the actual maker – of experimental explosive devices. This was a massive achievement.

"We need to go in there, now, and arrest them," May stated in a low, firm voice.

Owen agreed. There was no time to waste, and the danger was not yet over, because whatever these two boys were busy with, they looked about to take further steps.

In fact, he revised that. There might be no time at all.

As Owen watched, barely able to breathe, the taller of the two began connecting up a series of wires to a large box.

Weird, sharp fumes were leaking out of a gap in the window frame.

"This is not looking good," May breathed.

Owen tensed as he saw the box begin to spark and fizzle. Flames ran along the wires, in the direction of the larger box.

"Get back," he hissed, grabbing May's arm. "I don't like this at all. Get back!"

They turned and made a run for it. Owen kept a tight hold on May's arm, knowing they needed to get distance between them and this experiment, and they needed to do it fast. He ran with all the speed he had, aiming for the nearby tree that represented the first piece of solid cover.

They only just reached it in time.

Behind them, with a massive blast, the cottage exploded.

CHAPTER NINE

The shockwave knocked May right off her feet. She cannoned into Owen and his arms wrapped around her for a moment, preventing her from tumbling to the ground. They both staggered back at the force of the blast, which felt like a physical blow.

Smoke belched toward them in an impenetrable, toxic cloud and May covered her face with her arm, coughing at the fumes, her eyes stinging. She held her breath, not knowing what on earth had been in that setup, but pretty sure that it shouldn't be inhaled.

Gradually, the smoke cleared, and May stared at the cottage in absolute shock.

The roof had come all the way off and was lying on the ground in a buckled, twisted heap of steel. One wall had a hole blown in it, with splintered pieces of wood sticking jaggedly out. The place was on fire.

The sound was still reverberating around the quiet valley, and through her watering eyes, she saw horses cantering around the fields, tossing their heads in reaction to the sudden noise.

"The boys! Cody and his friend!" she said in horror, as her bludgeoned mind caught up with events.

Hastily, Owen let go of her and they paced cautiously back toward the cottage. May felt deeply concerned for the two people who'd been inside, and worried they might have died in the blast. But at the same time, she was equally worried there might be a second explosion.

She felt her heart skip with relief as, through the gap in the wall, a fire-suited figure staggered out, stumbling over the loose debris, coughing as he felt blindly in front of him. His helmet visor was cracked and blackened, effectively blindfolding him, May saw.

"This way, bro," he called in a hoarse voice.

In a moment, the other figure appeared, scrambling over the debris, but looking miraculously unhurt.

May rushed forward.

"Get away from there!" she yelled. She had no idea if there would be further explosions, or what else was wired up.

She grabbed one of the men, feeling the heat of his smoldering coat.

The other man's helmet had been dislodged, and his hair was on fire, May saw, as he stumbled closer.

"We need to put that out!" Owen shouted. Quickly, he removed his jacket and swathed the man's head in it.

A singed smell was added to the medley of aromas, most of them toxic. Deep black smoke was now belching from the cabin.

As fast as she could, May dragged the young man, who seemed half-stunned by the explosion, away from the danger zone. She got him about thirty yards away before he tripped over a tree root and they both sprawled down onto the lush grass.

"Turn around," she said, gently pushing him down as he struggled to rise. She started checking him over, praying that he wasn't hurt too badly.

"I'm alive!" he shouted hoarsely in excitement. "I'm alive! Wow, what a bang!"

Owen was examining the other young man, who was still lying on the ground, coughing and spluttering.

"Keep an eye on him," May called to him over the crackle of the flames.

And then, she saw a lavender-shirted figure marching up toward them from the main house.

"Cody!" his mother yelled, making a beeline for the man in May's protective grasp. "What the hell have you been up to? I told you when the school suspended you - no more science experiments! You could easily have injured one of the horses with that reckless behavior! Look how spooked they are!"

She stared down at him, observing his soot-smudged face, tousled blonde hair, and smoldering clothes. "And you could have been hurt, also," she admitted angrily. "Are you okay?"

"I - I'm fine, Mom," he husked. "So is Ethan, I - I think."

"Yeah," the other figure groaned. "I'm okay. I think my hair was on fire, but the policeman put it out. I'm not sure we did that right. I think it should have been wire A into slot B, not the other way around."

"Yeah, yeah, I think we might have gone wrong there. That's a shame, because it was proceeding well otherwise."

Swiftly, May put a stop to the post-explosion analysis. "You two need to come to the police station. We are going to formally question you in connection with recent crimes and your activities in the cottage."

"What?" Cody yelled. "You can't take us in! We're innocent!"

May noted how upset he looked. It was as if, in a moment, he'd changed character completely and was now bristling with defensiveness.

She glanced firmly at Cody's mother, expecting that she might leap to her son's defense. But it seemed that after the explosion, she was done with him.

"Take him away. Just make sure he has some means of calling me when you're done, seeing he's probably destroyed his phone. There's no rush," she said meaningfully. "Take your time with him."

"Mom!" Cody protested, but she was clearly deaf to his pleas.

"We will inform you when we're finished," May promised. "And we'll call the emergency services here immediately to extinguish the fire."

"Thank you," the woman snapped.

She turned away and stomped back up to the house, turning around to shout, "And if you think your father's going to rebuild your cottage a second time, think again! Once was enough! You're moving back to the house after this. And no more science experiments."

Cody let out a disappointed sigh.

May helped him to his feet.

Never mind no more science experiments. There might be no more life outside of a prison cell if this man was their killer. She felt resolute at the thought of the questioning ahead.

Owen had gotten on the phone while May was talking to Cody's mother, calling the fire department and the local police. He'd finished those calls, she saw, and was putting his phone away.

"Come on, let's get you away from this scene," she said.

May practically had to drag the reluctant Cody up the hill. Finally, she got both of them into the back of her car, which began smelling strongly of charred clothing.

"Okay, you two are going to come with us to the police department and answer some questions. We want to hear everything you can tell us about your activities over the last few days, and your history of making explosive devices."

Only stony silence greeted her words, and she sensed she had two highly uncooperative suspects. This was going to be a tough interrogation, she had no doubt.

May started the car and drove to the closest police department, which was in the town of Willow. It was a ten-minute drive away, and as she drove, she was forced to open the windows. It was very smoky in the car still. In fact, May thought she might need to get her treasured ride detailed tomorrow.

But having a car that stank of smoke would be a minor setback if they had the killer in custody. And based on the evidence, the likelihood was strong.

They arrived at the Willow police department, where May and Owen helped Cody and Ethan out of the car. This police department was on the main street of the small town. At this hour, just before four p.m., there was some traffic on the road and a few pedestrians on foot.

A few people stopped and stared curiously at the disheveled and charred young men as May escorted them inside. She heard a squeal of brakes from the road beyond as a driver took in the scene.

"Good afternoon, Fred. Can we use one of your interview rooms?" she asked the officer at the front desk, a young policeman that she had met a few times in the past.

"Afternoon, May and Owen. Sure, you can."

The officer looked as if he had lots of questions, but was making a big effort not to waste their time by asking them.

At that moment, May's phone began ringing.

"It's Kerry on the line. I'd better take it quick," she said, wondering if Kerry had made any progress on her side.

"I'll get these two into the interview room," Owen said.

Releasing Cody's arm, May quickly walked down the corridor to take the call in private.

Kerry sounded breezy and confident.

"Hi, sis. Just checking in with you. We're wrapping up here with the forensic analysis of the scene. Unfortunately, the email address is a dead-end for now, as the holding company is outside the U.S. and they're being obstructive about releasing information. We're going to have to get lawyers involved, and escalate it internationally. Have you made any progress?"

"Yes. We picked up a link between two of the earlier cases," May said. "We found a suspect, Cody Meyers, with connections to two of the past victims. He was busy rigging up an explosive device in his cottage when we arrived. It actually blew up when we were on site. We've arrested him and his friend, and they're both at the Willow police department. We're about to question them."

"Oh, you can't do that now," Kerry snapped. "You need to wait."

May felt shocked. "What? Why not?" she asked, confused.

"Interrogation of a suspect is the FBI's responsibility," Kerry insisted. "You must hold off, and wait until we get there."

"But - but we just brought them in! We could at least make a start. Time is such an important factor right now. Every second counts," May protested, feeling indignation rising inside her at this dismissive treatment.

Kerry's tone was adamant. "This is a high profile case. It's a national emergency. FBI must be on scene for the questioning of such a strong suspect. It can't be left to the local police."

"What?" May bristled all over at that statement but Kerry steamrollered on.

"So, unfortunately, there's no room for negotiation here." She sounded satisfied to be giving the ultimatum. "Step away. Leave them be. Get some coffee, and make sure the room is correctly prepared. We'll be there in - in twenty minutes, if we drive fast. Come on, Adams."

Coffee? She was more than a coffee maker! May was seething, ready to shout out an angry retaliation to that insulting order. But abruptly, Kerry disconnected, leaving no room for further argument.

She'd gotten in the last word. May hated it when that happened. And she hated even more that Kerry was using her authority – or rather, misusing it - to take over what should have been May's responsibility.

May was so mad she felt as if smoke was coming out of her ears as she stomped back to the interview room to tell Owen he had to leave.

This was unfair all the way, but she couldn't complain.

If the killer was caught, the case would be solved and Kerry would get the credit, even though May and Owen had made the connection, and put themselves at risk making the arrest. And worse still, if this suspect wasn't the killer, then Kerry had wasted valuable time, which the real killer might be spending planning his next scenario.

It was unfair and wrong, but there was nothing she could do.

All she could do now was prepare herself for the ultimate humiliation of having Kerry ace the interview, and crush the suspect's protests, and pinpoint him beyond doubt as the killer.

May wasn't looking forward to the next hour. Not at all.

CHAPTER TEN

May felt emotions boiling inside her as she watched Kerry jump out of the unmarked police vehicle, with Adams leaping from the passenger seat. Shoulder to shoulder they marched along the street toward the Willow police department entrance.

Watching from the lobby, she felt small and useless and thoroughly frustrated. The worst-case scenario was playing out. Her sister was taking control of the case, and insisting on doing every important step herself.

Make coffee? Righteous indignation surged inside her all over again. That was a low blow. It had been mean and insulting of Kerry, and totally unnecessary. She'd done it to be hurtful, May was sure.

And May knew that she, too, could get the answers that were needed. In fact, with local knowledge, she might be able to provide insights that Kerry could not.

Despite the fact that May and Owen had done some very intelligent research, found a common thread, located a suspect as he was in the process of illegal activities, and just survived a potentially lethal bomb blast - despite all of that, Kerry was taking over the questioning?

Really? Did FBI protocols genuinely dictate that?

She was being so overprotective about this case that May suddenly realized it almost felt as if Kerry was - would jealous be the right word, she wondered, confused. Could Kerry possibly be jealous of anything May did? Was that even feasible when she, herself, was such a top achiever? Did she really resent that May had gotten a step ahead on this case, and brought in a strong suspect?

Thinking of it, May felt incredulity bubble up inside her. Surely it wasn't possible.

Beside her, she heard Owen give a faint snort of disapproval as the black-clad duo marched to the doorway.

"You know, I don't think this is fair, or a good use of time," he muttered to May. "We've been sitting here twiddling our thumbs and being told to make coffee when we could already have gotten well into the questioning. If this guy's innocent, Kerry's just wasted a trip. And doubled up on resources."

Owen definitely sounded angry. Now, May had to put her own frustration aside and calm him, because having an irate team member would not be good for anyone.

She muttered back, "If it's FBI protocol then we have to accept it. Kerry might also be simply following orders. The main thing is to find the killer, right?"

Her voice resounded with fake positivity which she was sure Owen could pick up on.

"Hmmm," Owen said.

May knew he wasn't convinced. She hoped that he'd be able to hide how angry he was. She was used to this treatment after years of living with Kerry. Now, as an outsider, Owen was seeing the conflict that ensued when sibling rivalry clashed with the pressure of a high profile and urgent case.

"Hi there," Kerry said. "We'd better waste no time. I think we'll pass on the coffee."

"That's fine, we didn't make it, anyway," Owen said in tones of fake helpfulness.

Kerry blinked at him, looking momentarily thrown, as if she wasn't sure whether he was being sarcastic or not.

May thought he was, and rather skillfully.

"Are the suspects ready?" Kerry asked.

"They are. They're in the interview room. It's Cody Meyer and his friend, Elmer Breese."

"I suppose we can question them together," Kerry muttered. "But we might have to end up questioning them separately if they resist. Anyway, let's get going. You can watch from the observation room."

"I hope you will be able to pick up some useful pointers," Adams said.

The worst of it was, he was being totally serious and not sarcastic at all. That burned May, as she stomped off to the observation room in silence.

From there, she saw Kerry enter, banging the door open and marching in with her head high. Behind her, Adams followed, gazing threateningly at the two charred and smoke-stained young men, before closing the door in a way that made it clear this escape route was barred.

Kerry stared at the duo through narrowed eyes.

Cody looked up at her defiantly. Elmer shuffled his feet under the desk, staring down at his hands.

"Afternoon, gents. Let me introduce myself," she said. "I'm Agent Kerry Moore, from the FBI. This is Agent Adams. Do you know why you're here?"

"We blew up the cottage," Elmer said.

May saw Cody kick him under the table, as if warning him not to start talking.

She had the sense this was going to be a difficult interview. Again, she wished she'd had the chance to test her own skills out in it.

"There have been a series of murders in the area related to bombs. You were brought in as a person of interest when the first one occurred, at the diner where you had worked. This was because you were recently fired from there. Now, we find you also have a common thread with the second murder. The victim is a teacher at the school you attended. You were recently suspended from there."

"We had nothing to do with those murders," Cody said.

"And we've never had anything to do with bombs," Elmer said anxiously. "We were doing a scientific experiment. We were trying to transmit matter."

"And so you did. You transmitted a large portion of the cottage's interior into the yard beyond. But let's stick to the facts," Kerry stated firmly. "Unfortunately, I see from this evidence log that your phone was destroyed in the blast, which means crucial evidence is already missing. So we're going to need your full cooperation now."

Elmer said nothing. Cody gave her a hostile glance. Kerry watched them as if she expected them to react, but neither said a word.

"You've been suspended from the school?" Kerry demanded to know.

"Yes," Cody admitted reluctantly.

"Care to tell me why?"

"I just made a mistake," Cody said, kicking Elmer again.

Kerry turned to Elmer.

"Withholding information in a criminal investigation is a federal offense. Why was your friend suspended?"

"It - it really wasn't serious," Elmer stammered.

"You're going to get in a lot of trouble yourself if you don't tell me everything," Kerry warned him. "You're under no obligation to protect your friend. That's a dangerous attitude and one which could cause you to go to prison."

"He - he did the wrong thing in a science experiment and ended up causing a small blast in the school laboratory." Elmer was brick red and now, so was Cody.

"So you were experimenting with bombs again?" Kerry said, this time directing the question at Cody.

"No! We were experimenting with an inter-dimensional transceiver," Cody said. "But we got the formula wrong."

May had to admit that was an interesting choice of words. It sounded like he was making it up as he went along.

"And you ended up blowing it up," Kerry said.

"Yes. I know we shouldn't have. We shouldn't have done the experiment at all and it was all my fault." Cody's voice cracked a little.

"Cody, how well did you know the victim, the art teacher Mrs. Flannery?"

"I was in her class," he mumbled.

"And were you doing well at art?"

"I was flunking it," he mumbled again. "It's not really my forte."

"What about the diner? Why were you fired?"

"I arrived late for two consecutive shifts. There were reasons. My car wouldn't start for one of them, and then the next morning, my mother told me I had to help round up the horses after they broke out of the field. They were heading for the main road. It was an emergency. But they have a no tolerance policy at the diner, so they let me go."

"I'm seeing a pattern here. You're flunking subjects. You're getting fired from your job. And you are creating explosive devices as a form of revenge?"

"No!" Cody almost jumped to his feet as he stared at Kerry in outrage.

"Down!" Adams barked out.

Cody sat down hurriedly.

"Your movements yesterday and today. Where were you?"

"I - I was helping my mother with the horses."

"All day?"

"Yes!" He stared at her outraged.

"Who are your witnesses? And your mother's testimony won't be enough."

"She was at a horse show in Hillside. We trucked through with the trucking company at six a.m. We then stayed at the show all day. There were several classes. I had to hold the horses, get refreshments, and do a whole lot of odd jobs. I only got back at eight last night. Then we had to go out to dinner with one of the horse show judges. They made me go along to that. This morning, I had to drive the judge back to the airport to catch a flight back to Chicago. I left at six a.m., again, and got to the airport at seven. I got back at eight. And then I called Elmer

50

and we got going with our experiment. Which had been delayed. Because of the horse show."

Cody sounded slightly bitter.

May turned away from the window, raising her eyebrows at Owen. He raised his in return, and she knew they were thinking the same thing.

After a promising start, this witness had fizzled out. He had an alibi for the time the email reply was sent to the police from the cabin in the woods. He didn't seem like the person they needed, although she was sure that Kerry would check back and go through his timing and where he had been for the two previous kills.

But she didn't think he was their guy.

"I think he's either going to end up in jail, or winning a Nobel prize. But I don't think he's the killer," she whispered to Owen.

"I agree. That's a fairly solid alibi," he said. "The email from the killer was sent in response to police messages and that IP address in the cabin was not faked or concealed. So that timing is a certainty. And that's too far for Elmer to have driven. I checked and double checked the police report."

"I've just had another idea," May said. The intuition came to her in a flash, while she'd been thinking back about those two reluctant and embarrassed schoolboys covering for each other.

"What's your idea?" Owen whispered back.

"I don't think that Sheila told her husband everything that went on in her work life. I think she might have kept some of it from him because knowing about it would have made him uneasy. I am sure she received a lot of threats. As a criminal lawyer, surely she would have? At any rate, I think we should check that possibility in more detail."

"Via the police?"

"Yes. The police might have records. And the law firm also might have kept a log of all the threats. So instead of listening to this interview any longer, how about we go and look into those two possibilities?" May said, and saw Owen nod firmly in agreement.

They tiptoed out of the interview room and headed for the door.

CHAPTER ELEVEN

The Bomber waited in the trees, smiling to himself as he watched the gray-haired woman sail the well-equipped fishing boat over to the pier.

She loved to fish, and spent most weekday afternoons out on Eagle Lake. He'd gotten a good idea of her routine. He didn't plan on making mistakes, so observation was essential. He had observed her for a few afternoons now.

This was the time she wrapped up, as it was getting dark. And that suited him just fine. He had structured all his plans around her schedule.

She was a hard woman, that he saw. Her grim face gave evidence of her past. Even though she was retired now, she had a lot to answer for. He knew that better than anyone.

He knew she was the one to kill. She was the next one he would settle his scores with, because she had been a huge part of the problem.

He couldn't wait to set his plans into motion. Silently, he watched as she fastened the boat, tugging the ropes tight. She was very familiar with the boat, and so she should be. For the past few years, being retired, all she'd done was fish.

That was going to change soon, though, because she would soon be in his sights. He was pleased to be going ahead with this part of his plans. This particular part of his mission was something he had looked forward to for a long time. Not that he'd rushed into it though. He'd imagined the best course of action for many thoughtful hours as he watched from the trees, turning scenarios around in his mind and deciding what the most seamless way would be. This was all part of the thrill, he knew. Waiting, hidden, while considering possibilities in his mind.

It was essential to ensure the plan was foolproof. If it was not error-free, he would be caught. And he would be caught if he failed. There was no way out of this. Not for him.

"You deserve what's coming to you," he whispered softly in her direction. "You deserve nothing less, after what you've done. How I wish I could tell you what I really think of you."

He'd spoken to her a lot over the past days. She had no idea, of course. The ironic thing was that the way that he had to action these plans, she never would hear his voice. There would not be the chance for that. Which in a way was a pity, but efficiency came first.

He knew well that every scenario he created now would be riskier than the last. Now that the police had been alerted, there was going to be no safe place to hide. But he wasn't worried, not when he knew he was smarter, faster, more agile, and more cunning than any of his adversaries. And he had so many surprises in store.

For this project, he would choose his time, and set his plan into action, and then he would be able to relax and enjoy watching the next step fall into place. But he had to keep things cool, to not allow his emotions to get in the way.

"It won't be long now. You could hurry up, and save me some time, though," he murmured, as she climbed onto the pier and began unpacking her boat. It was almost dark now. The lights glimmered off the calm waters. It was a beautiful evening. Especially for what he had in mind. He was going to light it up still further, once he had her. And he meant that in a very literal way. He drew in a satisfied breath as he thought about it.

Finally, she wrapped up her equipment and headed along the pier, turning in the direction of the parking lot.

He ducked back behind the tree and waited, keeping as still as possible, because she had to pass right by him in order to reach the car. That gave him a thrill, knowing she was walking so close to him. If she could sense his thoughts, she'd run a mile. Just as well she couldn't.

But she strolled by him, unaware. She wasn't smiling, but that fact didn't surprise the Bomber. What reason did she have to smile? She was a true monster. Everyone knew that.

Quickly, he ran through the scenario in his mind once more, making sure he had everything he needed for this capture, because now it was time. Because of the logistics, he was going to do this one differently. He could not risk a struggle, or to have this woman alerting others.

He crept forward, waiting. She was on the phone now and that was not part of his plans. She was snapping out words angrily, as if she was in conflict with whoever she was speaking to. Not surprising. It showed her rotten character. Greedy, money-grasping woman.

That was who she was. She was full of anger. The only time she seemed to be at peace was when she was out on the lake, troubling the fish.

But he would need her phone, so it was good to see that he could easily grab it.

Now. This was the time. He watched as she reached the car, and bent over to open the trunk. There was nobody else around. In the evenings, at this part of the lake, there seldom was, but yesterday there had been, and so he'd postponed his plans. He had to be able to do what he needed with no witnesses.

Moving fast, he burst from his cover and sprang forward, grabbing her throat. This was the key part of the capture. Speed was vital. A scream now might ruin his plans, and then it would all be over.

He was stronger than she was and he was more than capable of handling her struggles. She tried to shout, but the stranglehold on her neck prevented her. And she tried to fight him, more violently than he'd expected, but he knew he was ready for it and could handle the physical toll it would take to subdue her.

He gripped her harder, and her struggles became weaker. Finally she went limp. She was out cold. In fact, she could be dead by now. That didn't matter to him. The lawyer had been dead beforehand, too. It was the scenario that mattered.

And he had her. It had gone perfectly.

The car keys fell from her hand and landed on the ground with a jingle. He bent and picked them up. Now, it was time to move her. This was the easy part, or at any rate, it should be unless he'd been very unlucky.

He checked around. He hadn't been unlucky. He'd always believed, in any case, that you made your own luck in this life. He was pleased by how cleverly he had planned, and how well organized he had been.

It had all gone seamlessly. The struggle had been no more than a blip in the quiet evening. It had caused no excitement and had alerted nobody who might have been within earshot in the darkness. This was the only way to make it work. He had to have every detail perfect.

He opened the trunk of the car and pushed her inside, making sure she was well covered by a blanket.

He knew he had plenty of time. It was all part of the plan.

And he only had a short distance to travel.

He closed the trunk and opened the driver's door. He reached for the key and turned it in the ignition.

Then, he drove out of that parking lot, making sure to keep to the speed limit.

As he set off on the main road, his heart pounded with excitement. This was it. This was the moment he'd dreamed of. The final stage of this plan was ahead.

He felt filled with anticipation as he drove her car away from the pier, and away from Eagle Lake, toward the place where he was going to prepare for the dramatic climax to this capture.

CHAPTER TWELVE

Twenty minutes after sneaking out of the Willow police department, May arrived at Fairshore. She and Owen had decided to do their research at their local police department, a place where the territory was familiar, they had their own desks and everything they needed. With space and resources at their fingertips, May felt confident there would be something to find.

A criminal lawyer who had a career history of eight years with the firm must have handled many controversial and difficult cases. May was determined to learn who had threatened her, and what the landscape of Sheila's job had really looked like. She was certain it would be different from what her husband had described.

They headed straight through to the back office, which at this late hour, was unoccupied. Checking her watch, she saw it was nearly seven in the evening. And there was still so much to do.

"I hope someone is still at the law firm," May said, quickly looking up their number.

"It's a law firm. Bound to be someone there working late, especially if they handle criminal cases," Owen reassured her.

"Let me get onto it immediately. Will you contact the police?" May asked.

Owen nodded, and May dialed the number straight away for Baden Harris Criminal Law.

She held her breath as it rang, but Owen was right. After three rings, a stressed sounding woman picked up.

"Baden Harris, can I help you?"

"It's Deputy Moore here, calling from Fairshore police department," May introduced herself. "We're seeking information on a series of crimes. One of them involved Sheila Craig."

"Oh, yes, I can't tell you how terrible that has been for us," the woman shared. "I was her assistant for a while, and it has just been so traumatic to deal with this."

"I'm so sorry that you had to go through it," May sympathized. "We are obviously looking for as much background information as we can find. And we were wondering if Sheila Craig had ever had any threats made against her in the course of her work. Would you know about that?"

The assistant sighed. "Threats? Yes, lots of threats. We're a criminal law firm. It comes with the territory, sadly. All the lawyers are threatened, very regularly. Sometimes anonymously, sometimes by clients, or relatives of clients, or the opposition parties in the lawsuit. Lots of it is just nonsense, but sometimes, there are people who take things to extremes, and we do take those threats seriously."

May frowned. "What do you mean? How do they take things to extremes?"

"They issue personal, explicit threats targeting the lawyers, or even their partners and children, their families, their friends. It's shocking what people can find out and how they can use personal information like a weapon. And as I said, it's unfortunately impossible to stop. We try to take steps against the worst ones, but otherwise, we all just have to live with it."

"Is there a record of the threats against Sheila?"

"Yes. We keep a complete dossier of all the threats made against all the individuals in this firm, no matter how minor."

"Would you be able to send me the information? It could be very helpful in taking this investigation further," May said, hoping that the assistant would agree.

She paused. "Let me check. I don't want to do anything without the correct go-ahead."

May was put on hold and waited, mentally crossing her fingers that the answer would be positive.

While she waited, she heard Owen conversing with an official from the local police department. From what she could hear, that was not going well, and May felt her stomach twist with anxiety.

It sounded to her as if the police department wanted to help, but couldn't work out how to make all the information quickly available. From what Owen was saying, it was sounding as if compiling all those reports and pulling together the information would take weeks, time that nobody there had.

One of the two ways forward must surely pan out. Now everything was resting on the lawyers' side.

With a click, the hold music ended and the assistant was back on the line.

"Yes, I do have permission from the senior partner to share anything that could help with the case. It's very distressing and as you can imagine, everyone is nervous they might be targeted next. Please do keep in mind that some of the information related to the threats may be privileged and may not be shared beyond what is necessary for you to identify any suspects."

May felt a rush of relief.

"That will be so helpful. I'll give you my email address. Can you send it as soon as possible?" She read it out to her.

"I'll need a few minutes to prepare it, and then I'll send it. I hope it helps you," the assistant said.

"Thank you."

May disconnected, feeling glad that they would have something available.

"They're sending a list of threats," she told Owen.

"That's great. As you might have heard, the local police who handled those threats just can't get things together in any workable timeframe. They're too busy there. The deputy I spoke to said that we were welcome to come through and look for ourselves. But the drive there and back would take a while, and most probably it would take the whole night or longer, going through the files," Owen said, sounding stressed.

"Hopefully the law firm kept better records anyway," May said. She was also very aware of the pressure of time, especially as it was now fully dark outside. Night was closing in, and they were still no closer to finding the killer.

At that moment, May's email pinged.

"Here we go," she said.

Eagerly, she clicked on the email and opened the documents that the assistant had sent through. Owen scooted around to her side of the desk, peering down at the pages.

"Wow," he said. "Those are a lot of threats!"

May scrolled through. In her eight year career, it seemed that Sheila had received literally hundreds of threats, mostly from angry criminals who'd expected the law firm to work miracles, but who had ended up doing time.

The words jumped out at her, filled with violence and intent.

"You deserve to die!"

"I should feed you to my pigs!"

"I am going to find you and run you over when I'm out."

"You should be chopped into pieces for being so useless."

May frowned as the terrible words scrolled by.

"I wonder how we can narrow this down," she said. "Perhaps we need to look for the modus operandi."

58

"You mean search for key words like bomb, explosion, that sort of thing?" Owen asked.

"Yes. If the Bomber had made a threat like that, surely he would have mentioned it? Seeing this is clearly how he thinks? We can at least try it at first."

May tapped keys, narrowing her eyes as she saw what came up. Owen leaned even closer, reading the words on the screen.

"He threatened to kill her with a bomb," he said, pointing to the first threat on the search. "He threatened to set fire to her house," he indicated the second. "And he threatened to blow her up with an explosive jacket," he said, pointing to the third.

"If we have to prioritize these, then to me, threats one and three seem the most relevant," May said.

She read on, to see who these threats were from, leaning over to Owen's laptop to search different databases to see where the threatening people now lived.

"Okay. Threat number three is not valid as the person who made it is now deceased. Killed in prison, I see."

"But threat number one looks valid," Owen said.

"Yes. I see the law firm made a note here that Humphrey Andrews, who made the threat, did so after being sentenced to ten years for blowing up his business for insurance fraud."

"Relevant again. The guy we are looking for clearly defaults to that mode to solve all his problems," Owen said.

"Humphrey spent just four years inside, and was released six months ago. So the timeframe connects, too," May said. "He could have come out of jail angry. Perhaps he planned revenge on a few people he was mad at, including Sheila. Thus the string of cases."

"We need to go speak to him," Owen said. "Let's see if he's a resident in the area."

He logged into another database, tapping keys.

"Okay. I don't have a home address for him. None on record, for some reason. But I have a work address, where he's currently employed and has been for the past three months. It's a used car company in Tamarack County, but they won't be open now. They close at six p.m. according to their website."

"We'll have to do that first thing tomorrow, then," May said.

"Yes, I guess we'll have to wait."

Even so, despite the frustration, May felt hopeful that this lead might progress the case.

At that moment, they heard quick footsteps outside and both jumped guiltily as Kerry's voice rang out.

"May, are you there?"

May jumped up, scraping her chair back.

"Yes, I'm here." She hoped Kerry wasn't going to get mad at her for having sneaked away to do some additional research.

"I need to speak to you. Urgently. And in private," she said, with a glance at Owen.

Owen stood up and walked out. May waited, feeling apprehensive, to see what her sister was going to say.

CHAPTER THIRTEEN

May felt nervous as Kerry closed the back office door after Owen had left. Was her sister going to chew her out for having left the Willow police department? Or was this about something else altogether?

For a crazy moment, May wondered whether this conversation was going to be about Kerry's upcoming wedding. Everyone had been drawn into the extensive preparations for this, whether they liked it or not. Was Kerry going to take a moment to have some wedding chat in private? With her sister, anything was possible.

"Listen, I've been meaning to tell you," Kerry said, turning back to face her.

"What?" May asked.

"That key you gave me, the one you found in Lauren's evidence box."

"Yes?" May said hopefully. This was about her sister. She felt vastly encouraged that there might be information at last.

"There was a delay in getting the label into the waitlist for the software analysis. I've gotten it in now and the techs will be analyzing it in the next few days."

"Oh. Oh, wow," May said. "That's great news, Kerry. Thank you."

With the stress of their current predicament, the thoughts of that key, which were usually simmering in May's mind, had temporarily been banished. Now they came flooding back.

Imagine if the blurred wording on that label could be read! Where might it lead them?

"Even if the software doesn't pick up anything, the photos of the key have been sent to a locksmith expert who works for the FBI. He's also been very busy, but he has some spare time coming up to try and trace it," Kerry said briskly. "So that's another avenue for us to explore. Either or both might work," she stated confidently.

May felt amazed that in Kerry's world, there was clearly no such outcome as neither one working. That possibility didn't even exist.

She felt a flash of envy for Kerry's superb self-assurance. What it must be like to be her. How much easier life would be without the constant worry of not being good enough, May thought briefly.

"Thanks so much, sis," she said.

She wondered for a moment if she should tell Kerry that someone had been watching and filming outside their house when Lauren had walked out, that she was sure Lauren had been taken by a person who had been waiting and planning for that exact moment. And that this same someone was now warning May to back off.

May felt conflicted about that, because in a way she felt Kerry should know and might even have an insight into who it could be.

But in another way, it might be the wrong thing to tell anyone until she knew more herself. Who knew who was involved, and the truth of it was that Kerry was living out of state, far away from any threats or retribution, whereas May was right there in town.

In any case, there wasn't time, because Kerry was forging briskly ahead.

"I think we're done for today. As you probably heard from the way Cody responded to my questioning and finally gave up the truth, that suspect was innocent. We checked out his alibi for two of the three previous crimes. He's actually quite a clever young man, who told me he wants to invent a better alternative to electrical power," Kerry said approvingly. "He just needs to learn to stop blowing things up at school, and to keep better track of which wires connect together when he experiments."

"Yes, I also figured he was innocent of those crimes," May said.

"We've wrapped up with the forensic examination of the most recent bomb site. Some of that evidence now has to be analyzed, so the bomb experts on our team will be working overnight to see if they can pick up anything helpful. I can't say if it will bring results. Unfortunately, it's one of those things that has to be done, but seldom leads anywhere conclusive. We'll meet with them tomorrow morning and see what the outcome is."

"Oh," May said. She felt it was a lame response but wasn't sure what else she should say.

Should she tell Kerry about what she and Owen had just been researching? May decided not to. Kerry had a morning meeting scheduled with the bomb experts. It was better for May to investigate on the side, she resolved.

"So there's nothing more to do tonight apart from my own video update with the team back in the office, two media briefings, and a few calls to the state governor and other individuals which I'll get to later."

May stared at her, impressed that her day would be wrapping up with these high-level briefings.

"Tomorrow we'll start fresh and explore a few more directions," Kerry concluded. "We're managing to keep the lid on the media panic for now, but of course, that panic will only be over when we have the suspect in custody. So I'll need you to stand by and be ready to help in any way you can."

"I hope we can solve this tomorrow," May said, feeling a flare of worry. She was extremely uneasy that this killer was still at large, especially since he sometimes seemed to hold his victims for hours or days before exploding them. What if he had already captured somebody else?

"I don't doubt we will make progress tomorrow," Kerry stated. "With the amount of expertise we have available, there's no chance this killer will be able to escape our net." She smiled. "So, I'm going to head over to the folks for drinks, and then take my team out for a working dinner to wrap things up before my final calls and meetings. Do you want to join me at the folks for drinks?"

May didn't. Much as she loved her parents, she knew it was going to end up being a stressful occasion. She would far rather have headed down the road to Dan's Bar, and had a beer with Owen to wind down after the stress of the day. But she could see this was not a question, but more of a command.

"I'd love to join you for drinks with the folks," she said reluctantly.

"Good. I have my own wheels now, so I'll see you there."

Kerry turned and stalked out.

Quickly, May rushed outside to the parking lot, where Owen was busy reading an email on his phone.

"We're done for the day and I have to go to my parents," she explained reluctantly. "Let's meet as early as we can tomorrow. Shall we say seven-thirty a.m. at Humphrey Andrews's workplace? It's a car dealership called Stan's Wheels, in Lakeview, so about twenty minutes from here."

"Seven-thirty it is. I'll see you there, May," Owen said.

May picked up a note of commiseration in his voice. He knew how she felt about family get-togethers that involved Kerry and her parents. But May's loyalty would not allow her to complain out loud.

She got into her car and headed off, on the five minute drive to her parents' place.

When she got there and parked outside, May found herself viewing the quiet street with different eyes.

Ten years ago, someone had stood nearby here, from a vantage point that she guessed was across the road somewhere, but could be further away. They had filmed Lauren storming out of the house after the fight with May.

That person had been watching and waiting. But where were they now?

May was sure it was not any of the immediate neighbors. She knew them well. One was a retired dental technician, now in his seventies. One was a nursery school teacher who'd moved to the area five years ago. And one was the local pastor's mother, who'd lived there thirty years. May simply could not see any of these good citizens committing such a crime, or sending such a threat.

It had to be someone else, but who?

Her thoughts were interrupted by Kerry pulling up alongside. As if on cue, the front door of her parents' house opened.

Light streamed out, framing her mother and father in its warm, rosy glow.

"Kerry!" her mother called in delighted tones. "How wonderful to see you here!"

May took a deep breath, preparing herself for the onslaught of admiration that her parents would now unleash on her older sister.

She didn't mind; she really didn't. But she wished that she wouldn't become invisible herself when it happened.

"I can't believe how serious this case is," her father said as Kerry marched up the garden path. "No wonder they called in the experts. I'm glad you're here to solve it now. People getting blown up, and in our county, too? Cops being killed? I can't believe what the world is coming to."

"Well, we know what an evil world it is out there but I guess we never expect it to touch us here. Come in, Kerry. You do look beautiful. So fit and well. I've always thought you are so lucky with your naturally fit build. You must tell me what you're eating now, you mentioned you have such an interesting low-carb meal plan! What a pity your wonderful fiancé can't also be here, but I guess this is a work trip and not a social one. And May, how lovely to see you, too," her mother said, sounding slightly apologetic, as if mentioning her as an afterthought had been unintentional.

May followed Kerry into the house.

It was immaculate. On the coffee table in the lounge, an array of drinks had been set out. There was coffee, tea, sodas, as well as her mother's famous non-alcoholic punch, with lemon and mint leaves. There was a bowl of nuts and a small tray of sliced vegetables and dip.

"What can I pour you? Sit, sit," her mother encouraged them both. "I was going to make cookies, but then I remembered they have carbs, so I prepared the vegetables instead."

"I'd love some punch, please," Kerry said, taking a carrot stick. "This dip is delicious."

"I'd love punch, too," May said, deciding it was the best choice.

"So, Kerry, I'm sure you don't want to dwell on the case, since you've probably been busy solving it all day," her mother said, passing them each a glass of the bright amber drink. "Let's talk about something we'll all enjoy and can participate in."

"The wedding!" her father said.

"Please tell me, sweetheart, what are the updates? Have you decided on the menu yet? And what about the flowers? Did you have a look at the suggestions I sent?"

Her parents both beamed at Kerry.

May sat back in her chair, sipping her drink.

It was going to be a long hour. She knew that she wouldn't get asked any questions and that this was all about Kerry. It always was. She didn't feel jealous, but rather not good enough.

She longed to be the focus of her parents' loving attention, the way Kerry naturally was. She longed to be regarded as the family's superstar and shining light, even though she knew that only one person would ever have that status.

But by tomorrow morning, May hoped, she and Owen could get a lead on the case. That was what was important to her now. Not her parents, not the wedding, but the Bomber who was now terrorizing their county and its surrounding area.

She couldn't wait for seven-thirty a.m., when she could take the next step in the investigation, and look for the killer.

CHAPTER FOURTEEN

It was a windy, cloudy morning when May drove up to Stan's Wheels in the town of Lakeview.

The used car lot was surprisingly large, she saw. There was a massive warehouse, with ranks of paved parking outside, where vehicles of all shapes and sizes were parked. At this early hour it looked to be open and busy. Salespeople were welcoming customers inside, and attendants were working their way down the rows, cleaning and polishing the vehicles.

There was even a man dressed in a yellow and blue mascot costume, with a fake rubber tire around his middle, standing on the sidewalk with a 'Stan's Wheels' sign which he was waving mightily.

Owen pulled up behind May and they headed inside to the large reception desk.

"Welcome to Stan's Wheels. Where can we drive you today?" the young, blonde receptionist asked them with a rather plastic smile, as if she was somewhat sick of repeating that catchphrase.

"We're police," May said. "We're looking for one of your employees, Humphrey Andrews."

Her eyes widened. "Why?" she asked.

"Routine questioning," May said. "We're hoping to get more information on a case."

"Oh," the blonde said, seemingly disappointed, as if she'd been hoping for a chase down and an arrest. "He's outside."

"Is he polishing the cars?" May asked.

She had seen on the description in the case file that Humphrey was a plump, redheaded man, and May hadn't noticed a redhead outside, but maybe she hadn't looked hard enough.

"No, he's the mascot."

The blonde pointed to the blue and yellow costumed man, vigorously waving the sign.

Owen spun around and gazed outside, looking surprised.

"Thanks," May said.

They headed out to interrupt Humphrey Andrews in his important marketing role.

"Excuse me," May said, walking up to him. It would have been impossible to recognize him without knowing who he was. The costume covered his hair completely. The blue and yellow hood framed his face so that all she could see were two green eyes and a puckered mouth.

"What is it?" Humphrey asked, stopping waving the sign and staring at them. "Do I need to move? They told me I was allowed to stand on the sidewalk if I don't cause a disturbance."

"No, no," May said. "We need to speak to you. We want to ask you a few questions."

His eyes widened. "What's this about?" he asked. Now, May thought he sounded nervous.

"It's about the recent murders. The bombings. We understand that you sent Sheila, your lawyer, a threatening letter when you were sentenced. She was targeted in one of the blasts. So we need to question you on that." May turned to the enormous car dealership. "Shall we go inside?" she asked.

But Humphrey took a step back.

"No!" he said. "You're just here to cause trouble for me. I'm not answering your questions and I'm not going inside with you!"

"But you need to – " May began. She didn't get any further.

The next moment, she ducked instinctively as Humphrey flung the large, cardboard sign at them. It whizzed toward May and Owen, borne on the wind like a giant boomerang.

She hit the ground as its cardboard edge whooshed sharply past.

Then the sign clattered to the ground, wafting slightly in the breeze.

May scrambled hurriedly up. Humphrey was no longer around. He was fleeing, sprinting down the sidewalk in his ridiculous costume, with the tire around his middle bouncing as he ran.

"We need to get him!" Owen said.

As one, they gave chase. May sped off, her feet pounding on the pavement, shoulder to shoulder with Owen.

"Stop!" May yelled.

Humphrey was not built or dressed for running, but panic was lending him a surprising speed. He darted into the used car lot, weaving his way between the vehicles.

People were stopping and staring. Attendants shouted in surprise as Humphrey blasted past them. One of them made a grab for him, but his hands slipped off the rubber tire. Through the window glass, May caught a glimpse of the blonde receptionist, staring avidly through the glass, clearly thrilled that she was finally seeing the takedown that she'd hoped for.

But what if they didn't take him down? It was surely unlikely that he could escape when he was dressed as he was, but what if he managed to hide away somewhere and get the costume off?

With a flare of worry, May saw where he was headed.

Humphrey had reached the end of the lot, and he sprinted straight out onto the busy main street beyond. Cars screeched to a halt, and horns blared. He was easily covering the ground, even though he was encumbered by his costume.

Hoping that she didn't get knocked down by a car, May raced out into the road, flinching as she heard horns blare and tires screech.

She dodged past a slowing car, and leaped out of the path of a speeding van.

In the morning traffic, he might just get away, May thought. He could duck down an alleyway and escape them. He could hop aboard a bus and be gone.

Or he could reach the end of the road and turn down one of the side streets and vanish, and they would lose him. She couldn't let that happen.

She put on a burst of speed and closed the distance between them, until she was only a few feet behind him. Then, legs burning with the effort, she reached out to grab his tire, feeling elated that she'd gotten close enough at last. But to her consternation, her fingers slipped right off it. The thick latex provided no grip, and was as slick as if it had been oiled.

Veering to the right, Humphrey dodged away and swerved past a parked van.

"I'll go the other side," Owen shouted breathlessly, peeling off from the pursuit.

May followed Humphrey, this time trying to get even closer so she could get a better grip on his slippery costume.

Lunging forward, her hand connected with his rubber tire again, and this time, she managed to cling to it and gave it a sharp yank.

Humphrey stumbled with a screech. Turning around, he kicked out at May and the toe of his blue boot caught her squarely on the shin.

"Ow!" she cried as she stumbled and almost fell.

Humphrey took the moment to turn and run again. He was approaching a row of parked cars. With a cry of triumph, he leaped onto the hood of a car, and then onto the roof of another one.

But Owen was keeping pace with him, May saw, sprinting along the sidewalk, dodging a group of commuters heading for the office park ahead.

Owen made a grab for his ankle and now, waving his arms in panic, Humphrey jumped off the car.

Across the road, a bus stopped. Its doors hissed open. Humphrey saw it, and ran at it for all he was worth.

This was her last chance, May realized. Gathering all her courage and speed, she leaped forward, grabbing him by the tire and tackling him to the ground.

He fell down, but the air-filled inflatable tire bounced them both high in the air. May gasped as they went airborne, clinging on with all her might as they rocketed into the path of an oncoming car.

With a shriek of brakes, it swerved, narrowly avoiding them as they bounced again, this time with less momentum. May realized to her relief that the tire had sprung a leak.

Now, she had purchase and could keep her feet on the ground. Humphrey let out a gasp of air as May sprawled on top of him, both of them bouncing gently.

He struggled, his feet kicking, but May had him now. She pinned him down and sat on his stomach, feeling the air gradually hiss out of the tire as horns blared around her.

And then, with a stamp of feet, Owen arrived. Quickly, he bent down and handcuffed the rapidly deflating mascot.

"Humphrey Andrews, you are now under arrest for attempting to evade officers of the law," he said breathlessly. "We're taking you in for questioning."

They hauled him to his feet, each grabbing one arm as they manhandled the reluctant man out of the road. Humphrey was puffing for air and his eyes were wide. May kept a death grip on the slippery costume. She didn't trust him an inch.

She couldn't wait to question him, to find out why he'd run in such a guilty way, and whether he had carried out the threats of bombing and destruction which he'd promised in such evil detail.

CHAPTER FIFTEEN

Standing outside the interview room, May felt ready for Humphrey Andrews, and determined to get to the truth.

After a struggle with her conscience, she'd called Kerry to tell her what was happening, in case her sister wanted to do this interview as well. But Kerry's phone had rung through to voicemail this time, which let May off the hook.

She promised herself that she was going to be as forceful as Kerry, and do just as thorough a job. No detail was going to be left out or skipped over.

She was most definitely going to find out whether, after getting out of jail, this man had made good on his threats, embarking on a killing spree using what was clearly his chosen method of criminal activity - explosives.

Owen hurried over to join her.

"May, I've found another connection we can use. I have just been reading up on the case that sent Humphrey to jail. And do you know, one of his arresting officers, Lester Biggs, was one of the two policemen killed in the recent raid?"

"What?" May paused at the interview room, her hand on the door.

This was huge!

Or maybe, as doubts rushed in, she realized it wasn't so huge. How could this man, dressed in a blue and yellow blimp suit, possibly have known who would go after him on a police raid? That would indicate an ESP-level of prediction, surely?

But maybe he'd targeted that police department, because he'd had a grudge against the entire department, not caring who he killed, but hoping for the big prize of his arresting officer.

"Let's see what we can find out," she said, opening the door and stepping inside.

There, Humphrey was waiting, seated behind the table. He was still dressed in his deflated blimp suit, although he'd taken off the headgear. Now, his flattened red hair was visible, shining in the overhead light. He glanced up at them mutinously.

"Mr. Andrews, you deliberately attempted to avoid police questioning. You fled as soon as you realized we were officers of the law, following up on a case. I want to know why you did that. Why did you do such a thing?" May asked sternly, sitting opposite him.

"Oh, yeah? I don't have to answer any questions," Humphrey said.

"Failing to cooperate with us won't help you here. You are in a lot of trouble," May pointed out.

"You committed a crime by running away from us and not stopping when we asked you to. Are you aware of that? Plus, you jaywalked, and endangered drivers on the road," Owen explained seriously. "That alone is going to get you jail time unless you can explain yourself."

Finally, that threat seemed to prod Humphrey into cooperation.

"I ran because I saw how bad it looked for me," he spluttered. "Do you think I wasn't aware of those bombing incidents? I knew what people would think when they saw you talking to me! Even my bosses have been looking at me strangely the last couple of days. Explosives. I mean, not everyone uses them, and nobody will believe that the destruction of my business was due to nothing more than an unfortunate gas leak."

"Really?" May asked.

"It was from a pipe that had been accidentally rerouted, and was followed by a minor fire due to an electrical fault that nobody could have foreseen. That ignited a quantity of plastic explosive that happened to have been stored on the premises overnight." He spread his hands innocently. "It was something that could have happened to anyone. I did the time, I took the blame. But now, I don't want to go back inside."

May stared at him suspiciously. It was not a good sign that he was already resorting to lies. She had to get the truth out of him. This was a matter of life and death.

"You knew where Sheila, your criminal lawyer, lived. You could easily have taken her. You knew about the warehouses in the area."

"Yes, I knew where she lived. Of course I did. I mean, it's no secret. It's in the public domain. And I admit, if someone blew her up, I don't blame them. She did the most pathetic job of defending me!"

He glared at May angrily.

"It's all so obvious. I'm the fall guy. I'm not a killer. I never went to jail for killing anyone, did I? And besides, I've reformed. I'm a blimp, not a criminal mastermind."

Ignoring his ranting, May stepped forward, and spoke in a forceful tone.

"You had access to the area. You could have set the explosives and you clearly had the knowledge and contacts to do so. You had the motive to make people pay for your losses. You had means and opportunity, and you tried to evade the police when we approached you. What about alibis? Where were you when the other disasters took place?"

She paused for breath and for effect.

Humphrey looked her up and down.

"It's obvious, isn't it? You think I'm the Bomber. It's typical. If there's a problem, it must be the guy in the blue suit. Let's blame the blimp! I mean, how come nobody suspects that it might be the guy who is really responsible for it all? You need to find that guy, whoever he is."

May was not going to allow herself to be sidetracked.

"Give me your movements over the past forty-eight hours, please. And I want detail."

Humphrey's shoulders slumped.

"What do you want from me? Do you want me to have a camera following me around, so that you can find out what I was doing second by second?"

"No," said May flatly. "I want you to tell us."

He sighed.

"I work from seven a.m. to six p.m. Only because it takes me nearly an hour to get into this suit, I'm at work just after six. I get an hour for lunch and two other ten minute breaks during the day. So that's where I was during that time, the past two days. Then the day before yesterday, I had a parole check-in after work. You can confirm that if you like. It finished at seven, and I then went to the bar down the road from the police department, and you can confirm that, too. I was working, I wasn't setting any bombs. I'm reformed, like I said."

Being at work during those hours did preclude sending threats from the forest cabin. May acknowledged that, but wanted to make sure that he didn't have any incriminating evidence on his phone.

"Open your phone for me," May said.

They'd seized it and put it in a tray as soon as they'd gotten him to the police department. It had then been out of battery and had been recharging on the side of the room.

Now, it was charged again.

Scowling at her, Humphrey opened the phone. He handed it to her reluctantly.

"Look, I know you'll think I've been a bit adventurous in my online searches," he said. "It wasn't me, I swear. It was a friend of mine, asking me to do research. That's what some of those site visits were for.

I, myself, definitely don't have a thing for spanking, or for latex. As far as latex goes, I can take it or leave it after hours. I mean, I have to wear it all day at work! Why would I be obsessed by it?"

May ignored him. She was only interested in his online roaming in as far as it related to bomb sites. But she was interested to see if he had any stored videos, or else if he'd sent any threats from this phone to the police department.

He didn't and he hadn't. She looked very carefully in all the areas where they might be, but found nothing obvious.

And his online check-ins had been activated, she saw. He had been where he said he was.

May felt as if the case was collapsing around her. This suspect had seemed so strong. So guilty. And yet now, it was all fizzling out, like - like an unexploded bomb. Discouraged, she put the phone down and left the room. And, as she did, her phone rang.

It was Kerry on the line.

Eyes widening, May grabbed it. Had some evidence been found? But Kerry sounded highly annoyed and rather stressed.

"Hey, sis. Bad news."

"What?" May asked, her heart accelerating.

"There's just been another bomb blast. I'm going to text you the coordinates right now. I suggest you and Owen get there, as soon as possible. Because this is now a major disaster."

"I'm on my way," May said.

Her hands were cold and her mouth felt dry. The worst imaginable had happened. The killer was out there, ahead of them, and picking off more victims.

This new blast confirmed without a doubt that Humphrey Andrews was not the man they needed, and that the real killer was still out there. All they had done so far was waste precious time on interviewing the wrong suspect.

She felt a sense of desperation as she rushed back to the interview room, to tell Owen about the latest disaster, and that they needed to race to the scene.

CHAPTER SIXTEEN

May saw the plume of smoke still wafting into the air before she even turned onto the suburban road in Greenfields where the explosion had happened. Thick, black smoke that made her stomach churn.

Owen, sitting next to her, let out a defeated sigh.

"I can't believe this," he muttered.

May parked behind a police car that had just pulled up. Its siren was still blaring, and then cut off abruptly as the officers climbed out. Two fire trucks were already on the scene, but it appeared the earlier fire was under control because the crews were now standing down. However, May saw that the ambulance crew was still working inside, with a stretcher being wheeled to what had once been the front door of a residential home, but was now a blackened and gaping hole.

May climbed out. The fresh, morning air was tainted with smoke.

The house looked to have been a small, ordinary, one-story building with a small and neat yard. Neighbors from both sides of this residential suburb were already crowding the scene, their faces shocked.

Two police officers were fastening crime scene tape to keep them back. The crackle of walkie talkies and the nervous chatter of the nearby residents resounded in the air.

"Whose house is this?" May asked, fearing the worst.

Her question was answered by Kerry, speaking from behind her.

"The victim is a Mrs. Philippa Jacobs. A retiree. Unfortunately, she was inside her home at the time of the blast, and they are retrieving her remains now."

Kerry looked calm and businesslike. She was wearing protective foot covers and gloves. "The bomb squad is already inside, analyzing the explosives used."

"How did this happen? Was her home broken into, or how did the killer access it?" May asked.

Kerry shrugged. "I'm not sure about that yet," she said.

But from nearby, one of the neighbors, who had overheard, cleared his throat.

"Excuse me, ma'am?"

"Yes?" May said, turning to him. He was a tall, gray-haired man with an expression of worry and fear in his pale blue eyes.

"I might be able to help you with that information. Mrs. Jacobs always used to go fishing in the afternoons. And when she arrived home, at about seven p.m., she would put her car in the garage. That's what she did every evening. But yesterday, her car was not in the garage overnight, but parked outside the front door on the grass."

"Is that so?" May asked.

"We have a neighborhood watch. They noticed it late last night, and again early this morning, and told us. We decided to see if she was alright, as she's an extremely neat person and this was very out of character. So first thing this morning, the control room notified her nephew, who lives a few streets away. He called her, and almost instantly, I believe, there was a massive bang, and her house blew up."

May's eyes widened. Beside her, she heard Kerry draw a shocked breath.

This sounded like exactly the same M.O. The killer had wired the bomb to explode when an incoming call arrived, and that was what had activated the bomb. And it was a family member who had detonated the blast, just the same as with the roadhouse manager, and with the lawyer. This made the whole scenario even more tragic.

May guessed that Mrs. Jacobs would already have been unconscious, or perhaps even dead, at the time. Surely the killer would not have risked her being able to shout for help in this neighborhood, with a neighborhood watch that patrolled and kept an eye out?

"That's very helpful," May said. "I appreciate the background."

She turned to Kerry. "We really need to find out more about these bombs," she emphasized. "How is he doing this?"

Kerry nodded. "Absolutely. We do. The bomb squad is on the scene already, as I said. Once they are done, they will analyze all the remaining evidence."

May saw the paramedics wheeling out a stretcher containing a body bag. So the remains of poor Mrs. Jacobs had now been removed from the scene. May bowed her head as the stretcher was wheeled past.

Then, May went over to the cardboard box and put on foot covers and gloves. She wanted to take a closer look at the scene without risking that she might erase any important evidence. And she wanted to speak to the bomb squad. Surely they must have something by now, some information?

Following behind her, Owen did the same.

May paced nervously into the shell of the building, which still reeked of smoke. She immediately saw that the bomb must have been set up inside the front of the house, which had then been blown out to the sides.

She stepped into the charred space. The blast had blown things apart, and the ensuing fire had worsened the damage. Charcoaled wood was strewn everywhere. Half the front door was blown into the yard, skirting boards were ripped up, and all the window frames had been blown out.

The kitchen was completely destroyed. May swallowed hard. The devastation was horrific. Had this been the lounge, she wondered, pacing into the blackened room.

The bomb squad had started work in the corner of the room. Two heavily suited men were busy, bent over a still-smoldering area. Glancing around, one of them saw May and Owen approach.

"This is where the blast occurred," he said. "Now that the body has been removed, we're going to be able to take a better look."

"Did you find anything yet?" May asked.

"So far, nothing much. I'm guessing it was a pipe bomb, which was triggered by a phone call."

May nodded. "Any idea of what type of explosives these were?"

"That will be determined when they are taken to the lab."

Owen was pacing around the room, stepping carefully over the debris.

"May," he said suddenly. There was a note of urgency in his voice.

"Yes?" She turned to him, anxiety flaring.

"What's this? Look here! It just started flashing now. I thought it was a signal enhancer or a wi-fi box or something. But then, I realized that there obviously is no electricity available in this place at the moment, after the blast. What do you think it's connected to?"

May saw what had attracted his attention.

Half-buried in the fireplace she saw a tiny, flashing red light.

"I - I think that could be - "

May's voice sounded squeaky. She didn't even want to voice the horrific realization that filled her.

"Another bomb?" Owen said, and the two bomb squad members whirled around in alarm.

"It must be another bomb! I think the killer wanted to blow up the first responders. We need to get out!" May shouted.

She had never felt such terror flood her as she did at that moment.

"The house is rigged for another explosion. Go! Now!" she urged, as the bomb squad team leaped to their feet.

Owen grabbed her arm and they raced for the broken hole where the door had been.

May felt as if the entire scene was playing out in slow motion. She felt as if every footstep she took was taking an eternity.

It felt impossible to move forward fast enough, to keep going. And the whole time, the flashing red light in the corner of the room, that now filled the area with its glow, was mesmerizing her.

It was a countdown. The light was getting brighter, faster.

"Go! There's no time! Go!" someone shouted. "It's about to blow!"

May sprinted for the blown-out doorway gap, her ankle slipping on a piece of discarded wood, but Owen grabbed her arm and stopped her from falling.

Would they reach it in time, and get far enough away? She didn't know. They were never going to make it; that was what she feared. But she had to try.

"Come on!" she screamed.

She felt Owen's hand grip hers tighter. Up ahead, she saw daylight with the crowds waiting beyond.

"Get back! Get back!" May screamed. "Everyone, get away from the house!"

And then, behind her, she heard a faint but audible sizzling sound from inside. The fuse was lit. There was no more time at all.

May threw her arms around Owen as the world exploded around her.

CHAPTER SEVENTEEN

May heard an enormous blast behind her, and a flash of light seemed to engulf the world. The next moment, she and Owen were thrown to the ground. May landed hard on the grass, with Owen on top of her.

Glass shattered and wood splintered amid the deafening explosion. The air filled with thick, acrid smoke that belched and billowed around them.

Debris scattered down. A block of wood hit May a glancing blow on the head.

"Ouch," she said. Covering her head with her hands, she cowered down, waiting for the fallout to scatter around her, hoping she wouldn't be hit by anything bigger. Only when debris had stopped thudding to the ground did she dare to look up. Blinking the stinging smoke away, she stared at the scene.

Owen was yelling something at her, but she couldn't make out what because her ears were still ringing from the blast. There was pandemonium around her. The crowds were scattering.

Owen scrambled to his feet. Grabbing May's arm, he helped her up. She coughed, brushing grass off her clothing. Her elbows were sore, and her head was still throbbing from where the wood had hit her.

"May, are you okay?" he asked in concern. This time, she heard him.

"Yeah, I think so. You?"

He nodded.

May looked around in concern, worried that the two bomb squad techs hadn't made it out. But to her relief, both of them were also scrambling up from the grass, where the blast had knocked them.

"We should probably get away from the house. I think it's going to collapse any minute, and what if there's a third bomb?" Owen said.

As the smoke from the blast began to clear, she could see that the house had been transformed into a conflagration. There was now a gaping, smoldering hole where the front of the house had been, which had now been completely blown away. Flames leaped high into the air.

Kerry rushed over, her face taut with concern.

"May! You're okay? I thought you were in there!"

78

"Owen saw the fuse light activate," May said. Her voice was hoarse and croaky. "He got us all out in time."

She was shaking. Her whole body was trembling with shock. She was aware what a huge debt of gratitude she owed to the quick-thinking and observant deputy. Without a doubt he had saved her life, all their lives, because that bomb had been well hidden until it had activated, and nobody had thought a second blast would detonate less than an hour after the first.

They stumbled further away from the scene as the firemen moved in again. Sirens approaching indicated that more fire trucks were arriving.

Someone leaned over the crime scene tape, and handed May a bottle of water.

"Here, I am sure you need this."

"Thank you," she said to the concerned-looking woman, blinking smoky tears from her eyes. She gulped gratefully at the cool water and then passed the bottle to Owen.

As her shock subsided, May found a blaze of anger taking its place. How dare the killer act in this cowardly way, killing not only his intended victims, but then deliberately targeting the responders to the scene? It was the most malicious act she had ever heard of. What kind of a sicko would do this, she thought, feeling suddenly furious.

May resolved there and then that she was not going to let this happen even one more time. Whatever it took, she was going to work out who did this, and hunt them down before they had the chance to kill one more innocent person, and traumatize and threaten the good people helping on the scene.

"How can we find out who he is?" she asked, almost to herself, but her sister overheard her.

"Well, it's clear that these bombs are being made by someone who is very knowledgeable, and who is intentionally targeting certain people," Kerry said thoughtfully. "The amount of research, and the cleanliness of the scenes, tells us that."

"But why a retired woman? What harm did she ever do to anyone?" May asked, confused. "Or is he looking to target vulnerable people? And getting family members to detonate the devices is the most evil act imaginable."

But as she spoke the words, she wondered if they might give her some much needed insight.

"This killer maybe has an issue with family?" she asked. "Is that something we could explore? It seems like it, from those actions."

"I suppose he could," Kerry said dubiously.

"He might," May insisted. "Maybe he is doing this because he has issues with his own family. So he's looking to destroy other families. Or at any rate, to let them destroy each other. It's been a common thread in three of the four killings. In fact, what if one of the killings was to take out his own family member, and he's done the others as a smokescreen? With the family theme in place to confuse the issue and distract the focus from him in particular? I know that the last kill wasn't directly related to family, but maybe now he's just escalating and doesn't care so much anymore."

Kerry considered May's words, tapping her finger on her jaw.

"I am not sure I like your theory," she said eventually. "It needs some work."

"It's just a theory," May said defensively.

"If it was true, then as an experienced behavioral analysis unit agent, I would say you need to look to the first or second killing. Because a killer like this would have started out with his own family, if he had issues like this. Or else, he would have done one as a test, and then gone on to destroy his target. From there, he might have been addicted, and then gone on to widen his scope. That might be why he's now targeting police partnerships instead of direct family. Because, as you say, he is escalating, and so any link is now a reason to kill."

"Is that so?" May asked, impressed.

"Yes. In my experience, that's how those killings work. So if you believe in that theory, that's where you need to look."

"Okay," May said. "I will look into the first and second crime more closely."

"I'm going to speak to the bomb squad and see what they were able to pick up before the second detonation. It could be that he planned it to destroy evidence he knew was already there." Kerry stalked off, looking purposeful.

Around her, the scene was still chaotic. Two more fire trucks had arrived with hundreds more spectators, all standing well back from the smoky, blazing scene.

May felt compelled to take positive action, now, to solve this. It was the least that all these brave people who'd died deserved, she thought. She would do it for the sake of their families, and for the sake of the community. And she would do it for herself.

"I like your theory, May. There definitely seems to be a family connection in the way some bombs were set up to be detonated when relatives called in," Owen said to her. "That's the message this guy is sending, for sure."

"Let's go back and look at the victims' connections again," she said. "And this time, let's examine it from the point of view that our suspect might have had a grudge against the first or second victim. That would be the manager of the roadhouse diner, Barbara Vining, and the schoolteacher, Mrs. Flannery. We need to look more closely into the background of both these two, and see if there is anyone related to them who has a criminal record, or who could have wanted to do them harm."

CHAPTER EIGHTEEN

It was difficult to get their car out of the mass of vehicles that had parked in a chaotic manner on the road, May discovered. She had to be patient, and maneuver her vehicle back and forth to inch it from between the tightly packed ranks of other cars.

She didn't feel patient inside, though. She felt focused and motivated to get back to the police department, so that she could take a close look into Mrs. Flannery's life.

May felt sure that there would be something to uncover by exploring the family connection that she'd picked up. Surely there must be?

Her mind was whirring as she drove to the Flannery's farmhouse with Owen.

She had to work out who this killer was. This man now had killed multiple people in four terrible and destructive scenes, and he seemed to be escalating. He wasn't going to stop. They needed to find him and stop him.

If he'd had a deliberate reason for killing one of the first two victims, and had then chosen the others randomly as his spree escalated, May couldn't help but feel that this was the key to unlocking the case.

"I know it might take a lot of work to uncover this motive, but if we do, then it's a certain link to a suspect," she said aloud as they headed onto the main road, ready for the drive out to the countryside where the farmhouse was located.

"For what it's worth, I'm on board," Owen said. "How are we going to investigate Mrs. Flannery's contacts? Where do we start?"

"I guess we start with her son. He will be at the farmhouse, I'm sure, because they stayed there together and he farmed the land as his business. That means they were hopefully close, and he would know of any family members or connections who might have been problematic in the past."

Feeling more and more hopeful that the theory might bear fruit, May accelerated onto the main road, impatient about the time it would take to get back to the out of town location.

Half an hour later, May and Owen pulled up outside the farmhouse. As they climbed out of the car, May felt surprised by how peaceful it looked. It was strange to think that such a terrible incident had occurred here.

She noticed there was a crew on site fixing the garage and rebuilding the walls. They were being supervised by a blonde man who looked to be in his twenties.

May guessed that this was Mrs. Flannery's son. She recalled that he'd had an alibi at the time of her death, as he'd been out of town for a few days, and had therefore not been a suspect.

"Good morning," she said, walking hurriedly over to him. "Deputies Moore and Lovell. We're following up on this crime, and wondered if you might be able to help us with some background? Are you Hilton?" She remembered the name from the case files she'd read through.

The son turned to them and she was surprised by the unfriendliness in his frown.

"Look, I don't see why I must answer any more questions. Nothing is going to bring my mother back. I've already had to suffer being a suspect myself. If you ask me, the police have bungled this whole situation badly. It's what, nearly a month on? And no arrests, I believe? Just more killings."

He sounded incredulous and May felt filled with shame.

"That's what we're trying to put a stop to," Owen said. "We're very sorry for your loss, sir. We are just doing our best to follow up on any leads."

"We didn't have all the evidence then that we do now," May said, attempting to help him understand why, sometimes, reinvestigation was necessary. "Sometimes, new evidence only becomes available when further crimes are committed. This is a very complicated series of murders. We're so anxious to find the killer before he destroys any more families. You'd be helping us so much if you agreed to speak to us."

She could see this young man was hurting, and bereaved, and ready to shut down. But luckily her kindness got through to him, and he gave a reluctant sigh.

"I guess I can help you."

He moved away from the activity at the garage, and May and Owen followed.

"Hilton, did your mother have any family members who had criminal records? Anyone at all who wished her harm, or who had threatened her in the past?" May said.

"I am her family. I'm all that she had. She was an only child. She wasn't a bad person. She was loving and kind and generous. She would never have hurt anyone, and she wasn't the type of person to have enemies at all."

"No distant family who were problematic, even anyone you were estranged from?" May checked.

Hilton shook his head.

"No, there was nobody I could even start to suggest as a possibility. Like I said, she didn't have much close family at all."

"Any of her students who you remember as being trouble causers? Even from previous years, or a long time ago?" May asked, widening the family connection to include her school family.

"Look, there were problem students for sure, and a few who failed her classes, but she wasn't directly responsible for anyone being suspended or expelled. Problem students were a problem for the whole school. And art's an optional subject, it is nowhere near as important as English or math. Flunking art is not a big thing. It's not career-damaging. So no, I really couldn't think of anyone who had a personal issue with her." Again, Hilton shook his head, and May could see they were not going to get the response they were hoping for. He genuinely could not think of anyone.

"I appreciate your help," she said.

They walked back to the car. May was feeling disconsolate. One of their two leads had gotten them nowhere. Kerry had said very firmly that a family member who'd disguised a personal killing as a spree could only have done it as the first or second incident, and that a killer would not have waited longer in her experience.

Now the only possibility left was the restaurant manager, Barbara Vining. And she guessed that the starting point would be Barbara's ex-husband. He lived in Oklahoma.

"Shall we call the police department and get the husband's details?" she asked.

Owen was on the same page, and knew exactly what she was referring to.

"I'll make a call right now," he said, getting out his phone and dialing Fairshore Police Department.

May opened the car and got inside, taking her pen and notebook out of her bag in preparation for calling the husband.

"Here's the number," Owen said a moment later. "His name is Sam Vining."

He read it out to May, and after mentally crossing her fingers, she dialed Sam. The number rang and rang. She was getting worried that it might not be answered, when finally a man picked up, sounding breathless.

"Sam here?" he said.

"Hi Sam. It's Deputy Moore here, from Tamarack County. I'm investigating the circumstances behind your ex-wife's death."

Sam caught his breath so badly it was practically a sob.

"I can't tell you how gutted I was when this happened," he shared. "I actually took a few days' leave from my work. I couldn't believe anyone could do such a thing to anyone. I mean, we were divorced, but not on bad terms. She was a good person. Are there any leads?" he asked.

"We're investigating any family members who might have been angry at her, and set the scene up to target her. I know she didn't have children, but were there any other close relatives of Barbara's who might have gotten on the wrong side of the law, or of her, in the past?"

"Not that I can think of," Sam said. But then he said, quickly, "Oh, wait, yes I can."

May felt her heart skip. "Who is that?" she asked.

"A few years ago, we fostered a young man for a year, when he was sixteen. His mother was in and out of rehab for that time. He was really bad news. He was a very, very troubled youngster. In fact, I think that having him live with us caused so much tension it contributed to the divorce."

"Really?" May asked.

"He had a juvenile record. We knew that when we took him on. We thought we could handle it and give him a fresh start. He'd started fires, exploded gas bottles, that kind of thing. His name was William Sime. I wish I'd thought to tell the police about him earlier, but honestly, it was such a bad experience and I was so glad to see the back of him when he finally got sent back to his mother, that I put it out of my mind and didn't think about it since. But here's the thing. I know he blamed Barbara, in a weird way, for 'rejecting' him even though it was the court's decision to send him back to his mother. She requested it. And, as I say, we didn't feel we were able to cope with him."

"What school did he go to?" May asked, wondering if the dots might be joined still further.

"He went to Woodbridge High School. Not that he spent much time there, between skipping school and getting suspended," he explained sourly.

Another common thread. So this troubled teen would have known the school where the art teacher was targeted. Perhaps that had made it easy for him to choose the first victim, before moving on to the more important kill.

"Do you know if William is still with his mother?"

"Yes, I think so. He would be twenty by now, so he might have moved out. But I can send you her details. Her name's Arlette. Arlette Sime. Good luck with her. We found her just as difficult as he was. But I'll message you the info now, and I hope it helps."

May stared at Owen, feeling as if they were on the verge of a major breakthrough. Barbara had fostered a troubled teen years ago, with a history of starting fires, and a grudge against her.

This provided a strong motive and could have triggered a killing spree.

May's phone beeped. They had the address. Now, to find out if it led them to the remorseless killer.

CHAPTER NINETEEN

As May drove to Dennisville, the town where Arlette Sime lived, Owen plotted the coordinates of this suspect's last known address on the map. She waited to see if he drew any conclusions, and out of the corner of her eye, saw him give a confident nod.

"Dennisville is definitely central to where the killings have occurred," he said.

"That is a hopeful sign," May said.

May felt optimistic about this suspect. He was connected to the second victim, but in such a way that nobody had picked it up. An old association. Years had gone by.

She wasn't sure why William had waited until now to commit the murders, but there could well have been a triggering episode. Perhaps even something to do with his neglectful mother, who had previously had to put her son into foster care.

Or maybe William himself had been in prison and had recently gotten out. There were all sorts of potential scenarios and reasons.

"May, I've figured out something else here," Owen said.

"What's that?" she asked, her hands tight on the wheel as she drove.

"It's not only family members he's targeting. Do you realize that all these victims so far are authority figures? That definitely points to a delinquent, wanting to take some kind of revenge," he said.

May thought back on the occupations of the bomb blast victims.

"You're right. The lawyer would be an authority figure. I guess police are authority figures, too. But what about the most recent victim? She was retired. Could he have made a mistake? Surely not. I mean, she must have been grabbed while she was fishing. He couldn't have mistaken her for anyone else."

"I actually spoke about the case to my mother last night, and she told me she knew Mrs. Jacobs quite well. She gave me some background," Owen said.

"And?" May asked.

"Before she retired, Mrs. Jacobs was a property manager. She had a very big portfolio of rentals that she was in charge of," Owen said. "She retired about five or six years ago. I believe she was a very tough businesswoman before that, with the reputation of being a battle ax."

May felt impressed all over again by Owen's local knowledge, thanks to his mother. A problem with authority was a contributing factor for a delinquent teen.

The miles could not fly by fast enough for May, and clearly for Owen as well.

"Here we are," he said, sounding excited, as they approached the turnoff for Dennisville.

This, May knew, was one of the poorest towns in Tamarack County. It was right on the town's western edge. Years ago it had been a thriving industrial area, but most industry had since moved to Chestnut Hill, which was closer to the highway.

This meant the town had seen a light manufacturing decline. Dennisville had suffered from loss of jobs, and had seen its population decline also.

May felt grateful that most towns within Tamarack County had a stable economy, especially since tourism played a huge role within the county, but unfortunately, Dennisville was too far from anywhere scenic like lakes, forests, or mountains, to benefit from that. It was set in the middle of a flat plain.

William lived in a three-story apartment block, which was next door to a row of warehouses and opposite a sprawling trailer park.

May noted, as they drove down the road, that most of the warehouses looked to be empty. This town had most definitely suffered a mass exodus of inhabitants and commerce.

They parked outside the apartment block. The walls were peeling. May spotted a broken window on the first floor, and saw someone looking suspiciously out of another window. She knew that the police would not be trusted in this area, and most probably with good reason.

Weeds straggled out from the uneven pavement.

"It's sad to think that a place like this exists in our county," Owen said. "I wish we could clean it up and get people back here. At any rate, I guess that's a thought for another day. William's mother lives on the second floor."

May hoped that Arlette would be at home, and even more importantly, that William would either be there, or she would know his whereabouts. This was an urgent mission. They needed to stop these killings, these slaughters as May thought of them. And fast.

They walked inside, where May breathed in the smell of rotting food, with an undertone of urine. This really was a bad area, no doubt about it. It was a place that could breed crime, and it looked as if it had.

In fact, from the looks of things, it was churning out crime, by the bucketload.

The elevator was so old that it didn't even have a door, just a gate that you pulled shut. When May stepped inside, she felt a shudder run through her body. The elevator creaked in protest and she could see that some of the wiring was loose.

"Maybe we should take the stairs," she said suddenly. That wiring was giving her a creepy feeling. It might mean nothing, but it was better to be too cautious than to be blown up.

"I agree," Owen said.

May felt a sense of relief as she walked out of the dilapidated elevator and headed over to the cracked staircase.

Climbing the stairs, she felt a sense of trepidation. When they came face to face with this criminal, she knew she would be facing a dangerous and highly intelligent individual who had shown an ability to preplan his crimes. She knew she had to be ready for anything.

It might also be that the mother would be difficult. She might know what he was up to. She could be in denial, or even enabling the killer. They would need to deal with her, to reach him, and that would be another challenge.

May and Owen arrived at the second floor. They walked down a dingy corridor, the floor dirty and the air stale.

She knocked on the door of the apartment that was listed as William's address, number 2C. There was no answer. But someone was home. From inside, she could hear the thud-thud of music. It was so loud it vibrated the door.

May knocked again, louder, and this time, the music was turned down.

"Who is it?" a woman's voice called.

"It's the police," May said. "We need to ask William Sime some questions."

There was a pause. A moment later, the door was opened. May found herself staring into the reddened eyes of a woman who she guessed must be in her early forties, but looked older.

Her brown hair was unkempt, with a halo of split ends. Dark circles underscored her eyes, and her skin was dull.

May guessed that Arlette Sime was still an addict, and had been for a long time.

"What do you want with him?" she asked, sounding belligerent.

"Can we come in?" May asked.

"I guess," Arlette said reluctantly. She led the way into the house.

As her eyes adjusted to the gloom, May could see that the living room was cluttered with filth. There were beer cans, empty cigarette cartons and dirty dishes strewn everywhere. The sofa was broken and the stuffing was spilling out, while the carpet was filthy. But there were some new-looking items. The TV. The big speakers on the walls.

Money was clearly available, just not being used for cleaning purposes.

"Is William here?" she asked.

Arlette pointed to the closed bedroom door.

"What you want with him?" she asked.

"Just to ask some questions," May said, not wanting to create any conflict, because in this place, she could see there was the potential for it to boil over, and with William so close by, they just needed to get face to face with him as soon as possible.

May walked over to the door and tapped on it.

There was no answer from inside, but she could hear a male voice, loud, confident, and smug.

"I'm going to kill you next, and you, and you. You're going to be bombed, sweetheart. And as for you, I'll blow the legs off your body. You know I can. You know I have."

The tones resonated with an evil confidence.

May felt a chill. She put a hand on the grip of her gun, just in case, not knowing what she would find when that door opened.

Taking a deep breath, she turned the handle, ready to come face to face with the man that she now strongly suspected to be the killer they sought.

CHAPTER TWENTY

As soon as May pushed the door open, William Sime, who was sitting at a desk on the far side of the room in front of an enormous screen, swung around in his chair to stare at them.

He was a tall young man, and although slouched in his chair, she could see his limbs were long and wiry. He had a shock of dark hair, piercing eyes, and a cruel twist to his mouth.

"What do you want?" he asked.

Disturbing as his demeanor was, May was even more distressed by what was playing out on the screen behind him. She heard Owen give a gasp of horror as he stared at the footage.

"The hell is this?" Owen murmured.

On the screen, May saw a young woman, pleading for her life in between two men who were holding her down. On the screen, another hooded man appeared. He was holding a knife.

The man with the knife brought it up to the young woman's throat.

"No!" May screamed, feeling a surge of fury race through her. The man was about to plunge the knife into her neck when the video froze.

May braced herself, realizing that this video was not yet finished. All that had happened was that William had paused it.

"It's a snuff movie," May said to Owen, in a voice that was suddenly hoarse. "He's watching a snuff movie. Turn it off, please," she ordered him, recovering enough to speak after having seen the terror in that girl's eyes. "We're taking you in for questioning, Mr. Sime."

She couldn't bear to stay in this room, in this apartment, a moment more.

William stared at them with a mixture of amusement and annoyance. He didn't look worried by the presence of two police in his dark, untidy, and smelly bedroom.

"Are you busting me for watching a movie?" he asked.

"We need to question you in connection with a series of crimes," May said.

William shrugged. "So ask me here. You're cops. Surely you're used to this stuff. You want me to play it again? What happens next is great. Educational for you, I should think."

"No!" May practically shouted.

William gestured to the TV. "Sure. If that's what you want, Officer. I don't see what difference it makes. It's not like I just killed someone."

There was a smile on his face, and a cruel glint in his eyes.

"You seem to think that killing is funny," Owen said. He walked over to the computer. With a quick, sharp jerk, he pulled the plug and the screen fizzled into darkness.

"Hey, watch it, cop," William said, getting to his feet.

"No," Owen said, turning to face William. "You watch it."

"You want to take me on?" William asked, a smirk on his face. "I could take you on. I'm stronger than you, and I'm faster than you. That I'm sure of."

Owen stepped forward.

"I think we could take you down without much effort," he said calmly. "But if I were you, I wouldn't get into a fight, because it's going to count against you. And right now, I guarantee, you don't need anything more doing that."

May didn't miss the threat in his words.

"You don't have a shred of evidence for anything I've done," William said. "Who are you? Some metro cops in some backwater town. You're nobodies. I'm immune to you. You can't touch me."

"We've seen what you're watching," Owen said. "It might well be relevant, since we're here to investigate the string of murders in and around the county. Murders involving explosives. That's what we need to ask you more about, since your foster mother was killed in one of them. Mrs. Vining."

May noticed that William didn't seem shocked at all by the mention of his previous foster mother's name.

"I didn't like Mrs. Vining. And it doesn't bother me to kill. She's dead. So what? She deserved what she got. You want to ask me about it? Sure, I'll tell you. I killed her. I killed the others, too. So come on, bring me in."

He killed her? A confession? May felt utterly shocked by the calm, amused words. This was not what she had expected at all.

He gazed at them, smirking. His right arm moved, and suddenly, in the gloomy room, May saw there was a knife in his hand.

It was a long, thin blade, shining silver in the dim light.

"See," he said, glancing down at his arm. "I could kill you. The both of you. I'll make you bleed."

"Put the knife down," May ordered firmly.

"Do you want me to?" William asked. His arm came up, the knife glinting in the light.

May got out her gun. She didn't want to shoot this suspect; she didn't want to injure him. It would delay things if they had to take him to the hospital. But this was a dangerous situation. They were face to face with a totally sociopathic individual. All that they needed to find out now was the extent of what he'd done.

"Put the knife down. Now!"

William was now looking from Owen to May, his eyes sparkling with an evil gleam.

"Say that again," he said, as he stared at May. "Say something else, cop."

"I think it's time you put that down," Owen said, taking a step forward, making his intention clear.

"Be careful, Owen," May said. If William used that knife, she knew what injury a sharp blade like that could inflict, instantly.

The tension in the room suddenly felt as sharp as the blade itself.

"Don't be a fool," William said. "I'm not going to let you take me in."

He jumped up from his chair. And then he lunged, swinging the knife at Owen's chest. The blade flashed in the gloomy light.

"Don't come any closer," William warned, his voice snarling. "I will take you out with this, don't doubt me."

May gasped in shock. Her finger tightened on the trigger. She had a sight on his shoulder. She'd have to shoot, have to wing him, even if it meant going to the hospital.

But with a sudden twist, Owen leaped forward and grabbed William's wrist.

He wrenched hard, and William gave a cry of outrage. The next moment, the knife clattered down onto the floor. With a swift movement of his foot, Owen kicked it aside. It went spinning across the floor, hitting the opposite wall, now well out of the sociopath's reach.

Before William could try anything else, May shoved the gun into her holster and grabbed his other hand. She dragged it back, snapped the cuff around it while William struggled, cursing violently, kicking out at them so hard the chair went flying.

"What are you doing to my boy?" Arlette screamed, framed in the doorway, shifting unsteadily from foot to foot.

"We're taking him in for questioning. He not only confessed to murder, but threatened us with a knife, so at this point, he's under arrest," May said.

"Murder?" To May's surprise, Arlette let out a hoarse laugh. "My son might be a killer but he's not a coward. If you take him in, you'd better watch your back."

May felt chilled by the words, but didn't let it show in her face. Adrenaline was boiling inside her at this tense encounter.

This man had not only admitted to the crimes, but pulled a knife on them. They had a killer in custody, and could now start to bring together the process that would allow them to close the case.

"We'll need to call the FBI. They'll have to be on board with this questioning," she muttered to Owen as they got William to the door, ignoring Arlette's cries of protest and shouted threats.

But as they hustled William downstairs, May couldn't help feeling a flash of unease.

Had he confessed too readily to the crimes?

Was he stringing the cops along - or could he possibly even be shielding someone?

May knew this wouldn't be over until the questioning was complete and they'd established his guilt beyond any doubt.

CHAPTER TWENTY ONE

"Well, we have our killer, I think."

May stood outside the interview room of the Dennisville police department, listening to Kerry speak the words in satisfied tones.

"All we need to do now is get a detailed confession out of him, if he's willing to give it. Otherwise, circumstantial evidence and a lack of an alibi will pave the way," her sister continued, sounding pleased.

This police department looked poorly resourced and the officers seemed overworked. The interview room had no adjoining observation room, the interior light was flickering, and there was a lot of noise from the echoing corridors around them.

But this space was all they had and it would have to work for them. Time was precious now. They glanced through the murky glass panel in the door.

May's gaze went straight to William, who was sitting, handcuffed to the chair behind the rickety plastic desk in the interview room. He was tapping a foot on the floor, but his face was impassive, almost bored. He was just waiting them out, May thought. Even though he'd bragged about being the killer, she didn't know if he was going to cooperate with them by giving the details.

But Kerry seemed more confident.

"We have the knife; he's been photographed and fingerprinted," Kerry continued. "It's all there for when we get his full confession."

"I'm not so sure it will be that easy," May said. Kerry raised an eyebrow. "I think William is smarter than we thought."

"Oh?"

"Maybe he was lying through his teeth, but there's something that doesn't seem right about such a blatant announcement that he is the criminal."

"You think he's protecting someone?" Kerry asked.

"Protecting someone, on an ego trip, who knows?" May said. "I don't trust his version."

"Well, let's drill down."

Kerry opened the door and walked in. May followed her, and William's gaze focused on them.

"Well, well, if it isn't the cops again," he said mockingly.

"All right, William, let's get this clear. You have confessed to the crime, but you have to answer our questions," Kerry said, sitting in one of the chairs as May took the other. "So do you want to tell me anything that might affect our work on the case?"

"Yeah, I did all those crimes. Bombs, right? I set them off. You go look at my science grades. I had the knowledge. And I made the opportunity." He laughed to himself and May felt a shudder of revulsion. She had to fight to keep her face impassive.

"We need to ask you some questions about the murders," Kerry said.

William shrugged. "I told you, I did them. I don't care about the details."

"That's a shame, because we do," Kerry said. "And you told us that you did them, but haven't told us why. Why did you kill those victims?"

William shrugged. "It's what I do."

"You've killed before?"

"Yeah."

"How many times?"

"I don't know. Six, eight, ten. I don't keep count."

"How did you choose your victims?" Kerry asked.

"We live in a small town community. I see them around, know who they are. It's fun choosing them. Like shopping, you could say."

"Did you think they'd be easy targets?"

William's eyes glittered. "Yeah. It's the way of the world, cops," William sneered. "I take what I want. I'm smart enough to do it. No one can touch me."

"No one?" Kerry asked. "What about the police? Or the FBI?"

"I'm smarter than the cops. And the FBI is a joke. That's why they had to send a couple of rookies like you. You're not going to get me."

May could see Kerry was annoyed by that insult. Seriously annoyed. This guy was getting right under her skin. But she was too professional to show it.

"You just went out and blew people up? How did you plan it? Where did you get your materials?"

"I'm not going to talk about details, no. You want me to give you a motive for the killings? I don't have one."

"Oh, come on!" Kerry almost exploded. "Of course you must. You killed people. You must have had a motive."

"Why? I'm smart. I'm good at what I do. That's enough, right?"

"How did you plant the bombs?" Kerry asked. "How did you build them?"

96

"Like I said, I'm not going to talk about details. I did it, and that's all you need to know."

"Why wouldn't you give details, then?"

"Because I don't want to."

"Do you have alibis for the times of the crime? Where were you late last night, and early this morning?" Kerry asked.

"I was capturing the recent victim. Mrs. Jacobs, right? I was planting a bomb in her house."

May shuddered. Was knowing her name and the timing the start of a confession? Then she reminded herself that William could easily have been following the news, which had given those details. They needed more to nail this suspect down. Especially since she was starting to think that he wasn't smart or disciplined enough to have pulled off such a technical series of crimes.

"Where did you capture her?"

"I can't tell you that."

Again, it was left wide open. They needed more proof than a broad confession.

May saw that he was taunting them with the fact he knew something they didn't. She'd seen this before - it was the attitude of a psychopath. He thought he was too smart. He thought he could escape capture.

But she didn't know if he was really guilty. He could be thinking that this entire situation was a huge joke. For someone like him, to mislead the cops could be a massive win; it could feed his ego. And jail time would only be a bonus. He already had a juvenile record. A guy like him would learn a lot in jail, May guessed. All the wrong things, and would be more skilled when he came out.

And in all honesty, it wasn't like jail was going to be worse than his home environment. Deep down, she was sure that William acknowledged that.

"You know, there's one problem that always gets in the way of our investigation," May said.

"Yeah? What's that?" William asked, looking interested.

"I don't think you're telling us the truth. I think you're trying to hide something. I'm just not sure what that something is. Because you're being vague on the details. So I'm thinking, maybe you aren't that clever. Maybe you didn't commit these crimes. Because if you didn't then you can't take responsibility for doing so."

That got to him. She saw it. May could tell that she'd struck a nerve.

His head snapped to face May. "Why do you say I'm lying?" he demanded.

"Because of the lack of details," she said.

"Details? I told you, they're not important."

"Where did you make the bombs?"

William hesitated. "At home, in the basement."

"And you've made them before?"

"Yeah, sure."

"Where did you get the materials?"

"I'm not going to tell you."

"How did you plant them in the places you planted them?"

"I'm not going to tell you," he said with finality.

"What supplies did you use?" Kerry pressured him.

"I don't use supplies. I made the bombs with household items."

"What household items?"

His gaze snapped to Kerry. "I'm done talking to you. I'm not saying another word."

"Why not tell the truth?" May asked.

William sneered. "The truth? I don't know what that is."

"Okay, I'm done talking to you," Kerry said. "But I will tell you this, you are going to go to prison for a long time. You will receive consecutive sentences for every murder you committed. You're going to be in prison for the rest of your life. No chance of parole, even with good behavior."

William said nothing. He simply shrugged.

"Goodbye, William," she said, sounding vengeful. "But don't think you've seen the last of me yet. I'll be back."

"And so will I," May said, feeling ever so slightly put out that Kerry hadn't said 'we'. But this was not a time for sibling competition. This was a serious situation. Something about it didn't feel right.

They stepped outside the interview room, where Owen and Adams were both hovering expectantly.

"Well, did you get what you needed?" Adams asked, as if this was surely a given.

Kerry scowled. "Not the way I wanted it. This guy is confessing. He's freely admitting to the murders."

"Great stuff!" Adams held up his hand, ready for a high five. But Kerry didn't reciprocate.

After a pause, Adams lowered his hand thoughtfully as she continued.

"We're getting no details from him. He's not explaining specifics. And in this situation, he should be. He should be proud of what he's done if he's confessing."

May nodded. That was exactly how she felt about it, too.

"There might be reasons. He could be protecting someone else," Adams suggested.

"Yes, that's the strongest likelihood. That someone helped him and he wants them to stay out of jail. Maybe he has an idea of controlling things from inside, keeping the crime and the killings going."

"Could be."

"But it could also be that he's a little sociopath who genuinely doesn't care, probably has killed or committed a serious crime before, and thinks he's invincible and that he can confess to anything just to waste police time, because he hates the police."

"That's what I'm leaning toward," May admitted. She didn't know why. Didn't know if there was a reason. But it was what she sensed about him.

"Or, he could be guilty and just have little memory of actually preparing the crimes. Which as you know, Adams, can happen." Kerry glanced at him and he nodded.

"Yes, I remember that case," he said.

"But given the level of detail in the prep, I doubt that is the case here. Of course, there's a fourth option which is that he really is the killer, did the crimes, is confessing to them to get a kick, but is not divulging the details in the hope that the case will fall apart and he'll be released." Kerry sighed.

"What should we do now?" May asked.

"Let's wait half an hour and then go back and question him again. And while we wait, Adams, you and I can go through the forensic reports of these bomb explosions, and speak to the bomb squad again. The more detail we have, the more we can use to trap him."

They marched off in the direction of the lobby.

May turned to Owen.

"I think we need to try and look for another angle. Another possible killer. If William is released, or inadvertently provides an alibi, we're all out of suspects. That's going to put our police department and Sheriff Jack in a very bad position with the state governor."

"Alright," Owen said. "Let's go take a look. I'm sure, if we scrutinize the evidence, something will come up we haven't thought of."

May sensed that they had almost, but not quite, succeeded in solving the puzzle. Now, she hoped that they were able to identify the missing piece, in the little time they had left.

CHAPTER TWENTY TWO

May felt the pressure bearing down on her as they headed to the back office to do the last minute research. She knew they were in a race against time, a deadly race. If this killer was not William Sime, and he was somebody else, then who was he?

As she and Owen sat in the crowded back office of the Dennisville police department, May felt at a loss to know which way to go.

The police department clearly needed more space. The back office was cramped, and from the piles of paper that were stacked on every available space, May could see that the filing was not up to date, and also that the case solve rate was lagging behind.

As county deputy, this fell within her jurisdiction, but right now it felt hypocritical to think of coming back with Sheriff Jack, and having a stern meeting with the department commander to try and improve things.

How could she think of doing that, when she herself had a huge unsolved case right in front of her, one that had the potential to do a serious amount of damage if she and Owen couldn't catch up with the killer and find answers?

They began scrolling through the information they had, sitting squashed up at a corner of one of the shared desks. Owen was next to a head-high pile of case files. May was next to a large, bulky officer who was slurping his coffee while filling in forms.

"Maybe it is William," Owen said. "Maybe both you and Kerry are doubting yourselves, because this case is so serious, when what you need to do is just go in there again and question him one more time."

"We can do that, for sure," May said.

Owen leaned forward, his eyes alight. "Maybe you need to appeal to his ego. To praise him and say how clever and intelligent he is. Maybe if you do that, you'll get him to confess that he did it, and how. So far, Kerry's been very dismissive of him, and maybe as a psychopath, he doesn't like that."

The cop next to May stopped slurping his coffee and glanced at Owen admiringly.

"Hey, you got an intelligent approach there, man. A lot of these criminals, they have big egos."

May also nodded in agreement. "When we go back in, I think that will be the right approach, Owen."

If only she had the same confidence that all they needed to do was to push different buttons. But Owen hadn't been there, in that room. He hadn't even been observing, thanks to the lack of facilities at Dennisville. He'd just been waiting outside, and because of that, he hadn't seen the way that William had responded.

If both she and Kerry were doubtful, it meant something. She and her sister hardly ever agreed! On principle, Kerry would usually take an opposing view, and argue it all the way down to the wire.

The fact that she and her sister were on the same page was an uncanny thing. If both of them were questioning and doubtful, that was surely a sign that there was more to this case than met the eye.

But what was it that was missing, and how could they find it?

"We just need to look at the evidence," she insisted. "If we're not seeing something, we need to try and work out what it is."

"Okay," Owen agreed cheerfully. "I wasn't in there. I guess I didn't see what you two did."

May felt extremely grateful for Owen's perceptiveness. She was so lucky to have such a clever, capable, and caring deputy.

As she thought that, her heart gave a little flutter which May could not interpret as gratitude. It felt like something else.

Which was unacceptable, because she'd told Owen that she was more comfortable keeping their relationship strictly professional.

May did her best to subdue the flutter by turning to the case. She was sure that focusing on the enormity of their problem would help settle her emotions. This was not the time to be worrying about whether she'd made a wrong decision in not dating her deputy. Not when a killer might be on the loose, and looking to strike again.

Who could it be? Where were they looking wrong, or where were they not looking at all?

"The family connection made sense to me," May muttered. "And the problems with authority, hence, the need to target authority figures. I mean, it all made sense, and we had the perfect suspect. Cold minded, and intelligent, too. But what if there is someone else?"

Suddenly, a thought occurred to May.

"Owen, what if the family connection that he's used means that this killer is doing his bomb blasts to try and get revenge for a family member? Not for himself?"

It felt so sudden, so right, that she felt goosebumps prickle her skin as she made the connection. It felt like a logical progression. They'd been on the right track earlier, but had just needed to widen the parameters.

Owen narrowed his eyes. "I guess that's a possibility. Where would we start to look for that?"

"I don't know, but maybe we must piece together the timeline," May suggested. "Because the property manager, as you told me, wasn't a manager for seven years. She retired seven years ago."

"Correct," Owen said.

"So maybe that seven year timeframe is important, and we should be working around it and looking further back. Because she would have been an authority figure seven years ago, and that might have been when the killer would have interacted with her. Or else, his family did."

"I see what you're saying," Owen said. "We need to go back further in time."

"I don't understand," the coffee slurping cop said, looking interested but puzzled as he turned toward them. "I'm a bit lost, myself. Are you saying this guy is looking to take revenge for something that happened seven years ago?"

"Yes, that's right," May said. "He's the Bomber. He's been killing authority figures, but we're trying to work out how he's connected to them and what the pattern is. Now, we think perhaps he's looking to get retribution for something that happened to one of his family. Based on the timeframe of the one victim's retirement, that would have been seven years ago, or maybe longer."

"Perhaps the guy or his family has been in jail," the cop said. "I've heard about the Bomber, of course. Tough, dangerous case. I wish you good luck with it."

He finished his coffee, picked up his forms, and headed out of the back door to his car.

"Owen, being in jail is a very good point," May said. "I think that cop just gave us a good direction on where we need to focus. On someone being in jail. A family member of the killer?"

She and Owen stared at each other thoughtfully. Owen tapped his fingers on the desk.

"I guess that means we come back to the lawyer, Sheila. Because she was a criminal lawyer, and she started her career what, eight years ago? Perhaps she would have handled that case, and that's why she was targeted?" Owen suggested.

"That will be the best starting point," May agreed. "It will be the easiest one to narrow down. In fact, it will be the only one we can narrow down."

She got on the phone, and within a minute, was speaking to the stressed but helpful assistant whose voice she now recognized.

"It's me again, Deputy Moore. I need another favor from you, please," she said.

"Sure. What do you need, Deputy?" the assistant asked.

"When Sheila started with the firm, I need the cases she handled from seven to eight years ago. "

"Okay, so basically, for the first two years that she joined the firm?"

"Yes, please."

"Sure. I can send them through to you. It will just be a summary of the facts of each case, the outcome, and any updates. In fact, if you're in a rush, it will be quicker to send you the complete list of all her cases as it's in one master document. You can then just go through it and look for the dates you need."

"That will be perfect."

May cut the call. "She's sending it as soon as she can," she told Owen.

She waited, staring at her screen, anticipating the ping that would mean the information had arrived.

It was truly their last chance, the only other scenario she could think of that fit the facts.

May knew they didn't have much time.

As soon as that email arrived, she was going to have to focus on it and try to identify all the possible cases that fit the parameters they were looking for.

Another minute later, May's laptop pinged, and she leaned forward eagerly, hoping that the information had just landed that would allow them to identify a previously hidden lead.

CHAPTER TWENTY THREE

May clicked open the summary of the criminal cases that Sheila had handled, looking for those that she'd been involved in seven to eight years ago. Her hands were trembling slightly from tension, and from the pressure of time they were under.

She scrolled through the list, going back through the years, forcing her analytical mind to take over from the part of her brain that wanted to panic at the sheer amount of information.

"Break it down into bite-size pieces," May told herself firmly. "Not all cases will be relevant. Start by looking for what is relevant. Make sure you are calm and competent."

Owen glanced at her as she muttered the words under her breath, before returning to this project.

Now that she was analyzing it better, she was able to see that there was not the mountain of information she'd feared at first.

Eight years ago, she saw, Sheila had just started with the firm. And because of that, her case load had not been high. She'd been handling a lot of minor cases, assisting with others, and had landed only a couple of major criminal cases to handle on her own. That narrowed things down.

"Okay, so going eight years back, I've got two possible cases. One was a big jewelry heist, one was an assault case," May said. She scrolled further. "Going seven years back, I have three here. One is a murder case, one is an armed robbery, and one is an assault case where the victim was shot, but didn't die."

"Those all seem like good possibilities. Let's see who was jailed, who's still jailed, and if they have any close relatives who are living in the area," Owen said.

This was a job requiring routine research, and May felt lucky that she was partnered with one of the fastest workers in the whole county. Owen's fingers flew across the keyboard as he delved into the cases, and then cross-checked with the other databases.

At that moment, Kerry appeared at the back office door. May got up and hurried over. Maybe she'd uncovered something important? But from the look on her face, May doubted it.

"We've found nothing that can help us forensically," Kerry confirmed impatiently. "But there is still further analysis to do on one of the sites. So it's time to go back in and question William again." She paused. "Adams had the idea that William might connect better with a male figure in the interview room, given that he has a very weak female role model in his life."

"That makes sense," May said. She saw where this was heading.

"Adams had the theory of building him up, you know, flattering him, praising him, admiring him, and trying to get him to spill the info that way. Which, as yet, we haven't tried."

"Owen also had that idea," May said, wanting to make sure her deputy got the credit, too.

She wasn't sure if Kerry had heard her as her sister continued. "So, given that space is limited, it'll be Adams and me this time in the room. Hope you don't mind, sis. I'm sorry you can't observe from anywhere, but as soon as we're done, I'll update you."

"I hope it goes well," May said.

Kerry turned away and rushed back down the corridor, heading purposefully in the direction of the interview room.

May felt deflated, but not surprised, that Kerry wasn't including her. Deep down, she wondered if Kerry also felt a creeping sense of anxiety to prove herself at all costs.

Could that be possible?

Did Kerry actually feel anxious, at all, ever?

It was a very strange idea and May didn't have time to consider it further. Instead, she turned back to where Owen was working through the list.

With the suspect interview now being handled by the FBI alone, this list represented their only hope of making a contribution to the case, and finding the killer if it didn't turn out to be William. May felt hopeful that Owen would pinpoint something they could follow up on.

She watched Owen as he worked, his eyes narrowed in concentration, flipping between his searches and occasionally pausing to paste a link, or jot something down.

"Only two of the perpetrators are still in jail," Owen said at last, with a sigh, straightening up and easing his shoulders back. "The perpetrator of the violent armed robbery case, and the perpetrator of the murder."

"Who are they?" May said, feeling eager. "Do you have more details?"

"The perpetrator of the violent armed robbery case is a man named Bart Evanston, now aged sixty-five. And he has a son!" Owen said, sounding optimistic.

"Who is he?" May asked, leaning over his laptop.

"Hang on, I'm finding out."

Owen tapped keys as May breathed down his neck. This could be a very promising lead.

"The son was also involved in organizing the robberies," Owen read. "It says here his name's Dave."

May had high hopes for Dave. She waited, holding her breath, for Owen to give more information.

But he grimaced, sounding disappointed.

"Not what we needed. The son's in prison, too. He was jailed three years ago for another series of robberies. So Dave isn't going to help us. Let's look at the other one. His name's Frederick Kane, he's currently fifty years old, and he has two children. Two boys. Dirk and Andrew."

Owen read on.

"Okay, it looks like Andrew moved to Mexico a few years ago. But Dirk looks to still be here. He definitely seems to be a resident in Minnesota, and he's twenty-four years old now. But I can't seem to find any further details on him."

Owen's fingers flew furiously over the keys. "Now, this is interesting. Dirk has a juvenile record. Sealed, but it shows he was in trouble at the age of sixteen, which would have been shortly before his dad went inside. But address? Nope, unfortunately those records are missing. Let's see if we can look him up online."

He switched to a different database, whistling softly through his teeth as he searched.

"This is very frustrating," he said. "This guy seems to be mostly off the grid. There's just nothing I can find on him at short notice, anyway. His last known address is his father's address, but when I searched again, it showed that apartment block was condemned and knocked down a couple of years ago, and there's no phone number for him."

Disappointment thudded inside May. They were so close, and yet at the same time, they couldn't pin down a man that most definitely was a person of interest in these crimes.

How were they going to manage the seemingly impossible, May agonized.

Thinking furiously, she came up with a possible solution.

"What if we go and ask Dirk's father? Surely it would make sense that he's still in touch with his dad, especially if he's committing crimes on his behalf? Which jail is Frederick in?"

Owen turned back to his computer.

"He's in Fallon County maximum security prison. That's what, half an hour's drive from here, just over the county border?"

"I'm going to have to do it," May said. "I'm going to have to go there now, and see if I can get face to face with him at short notice."

Owen looked doubtful. "You think they'll let you?"

May shrugged. "There's one factor I think could tip the balance for us, and that's if the FBI intervenes. So I'm going to start driving to the prison now. Will you wait outside the interview room, and grab Kerry as soon as she takes a break, or else if you're feeling really brave, interrupt her? Tell her we need all the powers of the FBI to get this permission granted, and make Frederick Kane available for questioning."

"Right," Owen said, his voice filled with resolve. "I'll do it."

With her plan now coming together, tenuous and risky as it was, May grabbed her keys and purse, and rushed out of the door.

CHAPTER TWENTY FOUR

The Bomber felt excited, breathless with tension, as he slunk into the basement parking lot below the main building.

This was going to be his biggest coup yet, and it had taken a long while and lots of planning, to reach this moment.

He'd dreamed of it ever since he'd been inspired to take his revenge. This was going to be a personal high point for him in his new career as the bringer of revenge.

Security was tight here. That was no surprise. Important business was done in this building.

Its gabled frontage spoke of its colonial origins. It was set among flower beds and topiary hedges.

But although the frontage was elegant and the interior was wood, polished and antique, it had modern cameras and surveillance; and visitors who wanted to proceed beyond the lobby had to sign in and be checked out.

But he'd gotten around it by dressing in the overalls of an electrical company that he'd seen the building managers use. And that also provided a good excuse for him to bring in the large backpack, in which his most powerful bombs yet were concealed.

Not just one. Oh, no. He wasn't stopping at one this time. He was going to make sure that some of the first responders went down, too.

But his main target was someone different. A key person in his life. The need for revenge surged inside him.

This woman had been pivotal in his father's case. If it had not been for her, his dad would never have been sentenced to life in prison for murder.

This woman had engineered his father's fate. Of course, nothing about it had been based on truth. Lies, lies all the way. He'd seen them. Those people had reveled in their lies.

The Bomber knew the truth about his dad.

His dad had been framed. Of course he had. He wasn't sure by whom, but he was sure it had all been unfair. At the time, the Bomber himself had been off the rails, drinking, running away from home, skipping school. He'd been arrested a couple of times. He hadn't known all the details of exactly how this had played out, but now those didn't matter. What mattered was the revenge he was taking on everyone who had been involved.

The schoolteacher who'd kept him in detention on the day of the murder for skipping class the day before. If it hadn't been for that, then he might have been able to see what had happened. As it was, he'd been stuck in a classroom when his dad had gone on this so-called killing spree.

The manager of the diner that had been opposite where the shooting occurred. That was where the victims had eaten before they got on the street and into the road rage incident with his dad, where he'd ended up killing them. Probably in self-defense. But in any case, the manager of the diner had been responsible. If it hadn't been for her diner, those people would not have been in the area and gotten into that conflict.

And the rental agent who had kicked his dad out of their lodgings shortly before this apparent crime had taken place. His dad had been furious about that. Just because he'd defaulted on the rent for months, didn't mean he wasn't planning to pay. But that harsh, unfair woman had given them no chance and had sent them packing, to live in an apartment block that was almost ready to be condemned.

Of course, the lawyer was a key person and one that he'd enjoyed taking down. She hadn't gotten his dad off. She'd been useless.

The police - well, the more police that got killed, the better, but he was particularly pleased to have punished some police from the very same department that had arrested his dad. The Sunnybrook police department.

He couldn't go as far as making sure they were exactly the same officers, but he'd done his best. At least some had gone down. A representative sample.

And now, the Bomber was going to punish one of the people who had been key in deciding his father's fate. This was approaching the pinnacle of his plans.

The petite woman, with graying hair and a slim figure was now in her late fifties, he guessed.

She'd had a long and hard working career. A defender of women's rights, a leader in her field. She had one of the best reputations in the business, and there were rumors that she would soon move from her current role into a successful political career.

But she wouldn't. Those plans were never going to be realized, because the esteemed lady was going to be taken out in a ball of flame.

He was only sorry that he hadn't managed to get to her earlier.

110

The injustice of his father's treatment was the reason that he had spent the last few years finding out all he could about this wicked woman, and planning this day.

She had been responsible for bringing down his father. It was thanks to her input that the system had taken away his father's freedom, his dignity, his pride. She had taken away the Bomber's family, his future.

As he reached the steel door that led to the basement parking area, he smiled to himself, pleased with the elegance of his plan. He was so elated that it was hard to keep control of himself. He wanted to laugh out loud and pump the air with his fists.

But he had to control himself. Even though this was special. This was a moment to savor. He had to remain calm and focused, or he might make mistakes.

He had a master key that the building maintenance department had been happy to hand over.

The Bomber had told them he'd been sent to fix the basement lights, and that he needed access to that area. The maintenance crew had handed the key over without question.

No one suspects the friendly neighborhood electrician.

He chuckled to himself. No one suspected that he was the Bomber. No one had the faintest idea that the young, clean-cut guy in the overalls was smuggling in explosives, and planning to use them.

He looked around, making sure that there was nobody about. He felt his heart pound, and a shudder of excitement went through him.

This was the day he had been preparing for. The day he had been waiting for.

He pulled the key out of his pocket, and turned it in the lock. He pulled the door open, and stepped through it.

Inside the large basement, it was dimly lit. The lights gleamed over all the shiny cars parked inside, many of them belonging to wealthy and influential people.

The destruction would not be confined to one car alone, and he felt a thrill of satisfaction to know that others she'd associated with would also suffer losses, and might even be injured and killed alongside her. It would send a message. It would show them. It would punish them as they deserved.

He felt the bag that he'd placed on the ground, and was reassured by the weight of the bombs inside as he picked it carefully up.

The bomber strolled forward, his backpack on his back, laughing softly to himself. It was exhilarating, intoxicating, and he felt his skin tingle with the excitement.

As he glided through the rows of cars, he felt his heart racing. He stopped in front of the BMW she drove, and grinned.

Hello, sweetheart. Soon, you'll be in a world of pain. But not for long, he admitted to himself. Only for a moment. And then, you will be no more. Exterminated, like a rat, in the powerful blast.

It was what she had earned, for the suffering and misery that she had caused to the Bomber and his father.

It was only right that she should die.

And he wasn't even going to set the bombs so that they were detonated by family members, not this time. For this occasion, he was going to do the bombs on a timer. It would be easy because this woman was clockwork in her habits. He knew to the second when she would leave her office, and arrive at her car. The video camera was set up and waiting near her car, ready to roll. It would capture and transmit whatever footage he couldn't personally watch.

"I'm looking forward to seeing you soon," he whispered to himself, smiling tightly as he prepared for the concentrated effort and planning the next few minutes would take.

CHAPTER TWENTY FIVE

May drove to Fallon County maximum security prison as fast as she could, her hands tight on the wheel. She had no idea if her mission would be successful, or if she would be turned away from the prison and refused entry.

It was a last-ditch idea, and it hinged on Owen being able to speak to Kerry, and persuade her that the FBI should intervene and allow this visit. Those things were far beyond her control.

And with the prison in sight, May still had no clue whether this mission would be possible. She hadn't heard back from Owen and had been focusing all her attention on driving, so she hadn't checked her messages.

Now, as she reached the prison gates, she stopped at the security booth and reached hurriedly for her phone.

Her heart thudded down as she saw nobody had messaged her. Not Owen, not Kerry. There was no point in her calling them. She knew that Owen would be waiting, just as anxious, for the permission - or not. And that as soon as there was an answer, either Owen or Kerry would let her know.

Perhaps, by some miracle, permission had already been granted, or her humble deputy status would allow her entry, May thought hopefully.

"Your name?" the guard said. The uniformed, middle-aged man sounded bored, as one would who asked this question a hundred times a day. But he wasn't careless. His eyes scanned May carefully as he reached for his iPad.

"Deputy May Moore," she replied.

"You here to see?"

She sighed. It didn't sound like her name was on the list at all.

"I'm here to interview a prisoner, if that's possible. Name of Frederick Kane, in the maximum security section."

May held her breath, waiting to see if her request would succeed, or fail dismally.

"I'm sorry, ma'am, but no one's allowed to see Kane, or any other of the maximum security prisoners, outside of the official visiting hours, unless they've got special approval from the head warden, who's our prison manager. Visiting hours for maximum-security prisoners are on weekend mornings only. So, you wouldn't happen to have that approval?"

The guard looked at her expectantly, his eyebrows raised.

"It's very urgent. We're busy with a multiple murder case. He may have information on the perpetrator," May pleaded.

"Ma'am, I understand. But prison rules are rules. They're put in place to ensure everyone's safety and cannot be broken. You'll need to get approval first."

"How do I get the approval?" May asked desperately.

"You need to apply to the head warden, with your reasons. It usually takes twenty-four hours to grant or deny the approval, and the appointment will then be scheduled the following day."

May stared at him in panic. He was sounding as if this was a good thing. It wasn't. Not with the urgency of this case, and the political pressure to solve it, that was intensifying by the minute.

"Is there any way I could speak to the head warden now?"

"Now? That's not possible, ma'am. He has a very busy day. He briefed me this morning, and I don't expect to hear from him again until tomorrow morning." Folding his arms, the guard stared at her with an expression that contained a trace of sympathy, but clearly nowhere near enough to bypass the rules.

"Look, could you maybe give me the head warden's phone number?" May said, desperately wondering how she could negotiate further. There was a car pulling up behind her. That probably contained a legitimate visitor and it meant she would be asked to move.

But, at that moment, the guard's phone started ringing. He checked the screen and raised his eyebrows.

Then he answered, turning away from her.

May didn't even dare to hope. She waited, with every moment feeling as long as an hour.

Then the guard turned back.

"Ma'am, why didn't you say you were deployed by the FBI, and that Senior Special Agent Keith Ross was calling the head warden personally to request this interview?" he asked, sounding puzzled. "It's authorized as a national-level emergency visit."

May felt relief wash over her. Kerry had organized an intervention at the highest possible level, and at the last possible nanosecond.

"Thank you so much," she said.

"Turn right, enter the security gate on the far right side, park in that area, go to the door marked 'Official', and someone will be waiting for you there," he advised.

Then he opened the tall, steel gate. It rattled back, and May drove through. She took the road to the right, which led up to another secure parking area.

As she reached the parking bay in the area near the stipulated door, her phone beeped. It was Kerry.

'Hope you're inside, sis! We did what we could. Let me know!'

May quickly texted back. *'I'm in!'*

Then, putting her phone away, she climbed out.

A uniformed guard was waiting for her at the door.

"FBI Agent May Moore?" he asked. Clearly there had been some miscommunication during this hurried arrangement.

"Good morning," May said. She wasn't an FBI agent. If only! "I'm actually a deputy, deployed by the FBI," she said, wanting to make sure everything was correct.

"I understand you are wanting an emergency interview with prisoner Kane."

"That's right."

"He's being transferred to the interview room now. Follow me."

He reached for his radio and spoke into the transmitter with rapid, professional dispatch.

Then he set off, marching along the corridor, which was lit by strip lights in the ceiling, and was surprisingly chilly. There were no visible windows, but May saw a camera on the wall, its eye staring at them blankly.

That camera reminded her of how the killer was filming his scenes, and it brought home to her all over again how important this visit was. May hurried behind the guard, hastily preparing what she should say when she came face to face with the dangerous lifer.

They reached a set of steel double doors.

"Wait here," the guard said.

He pushed open a door beside the one marked 'Official', and checked inside, speaking to somebody in the next room.

After a moment, the guard closed the door.

"He's on the way," he reported. "I'll need you to wait here a few moments, ma'am."

"Thank you," May replied, feeling nervousness crawl through her. She shifted from foot to foot, feeling her anxiety surge. Up until now, she'd been too relieved at getting inside to be scared. Now, she was realizing the enormity of her responsibility, and how much rode on getting a result.

It could be make or break. He could know something or nothing. But finding it out would depend on her.

Beyond the door, she heard the clanging of steel gates, the tramp of footsteps, and the murmur of men's voices. Just an ordinary day in the maximum security prison, though for her, an extraordinary one.

The door opened, and a prison warden hurried out.

"They are ready for you, Agent Moore," he said. "I'll escort you from here. Please, follow me."

It seemed there was no getting away from her temporary promotion to an FBI agent. May stepped through the door. She found herself in a long room that she guessed was used for the official meeting room on days when the prisoners were allowed visitors.

It had booths, with security glass and chairs on either side, and phones so that the prisoners could communicate with their visitors.

But the warden led her past this room, and into an annex that had a steel table across its length, with two chairs on either side.

"For this interview, given its importance, we thought you should be face to face. This room is fully monitored and there is camera surveillance, but we'll leave you alone with Kane if you're comfortable. He will be in cuffs and leg irons, of course."

"Yes, I'm comfortable," May said. She could hear the quiver in her own voice. She hoped he couldn't hear it. But this meant so much.

"Please, sit. He'll be through in a moment. I'm right outside."

The warden closed the door, leaving May alone in the small room with its blank walls and harsh overhead light, that smelled of disinfectant.

And then, the door on the far end opened and she felt her heart speed up even more.

Prisoner Kane was walking in.

CHAPTER TWENTY SIX

May's heart pounded as she stared at this prisoner, who might hold the key that could unlock the entire case, if she could only ask him the right questions.

If he was prepared to answer them. If he was in the right mood, or if he even liked or respected her enough to want to.

He shuffled in. Leg irons restricted his movements, and his hands were cuffed in front of him.

He was a tall, rangy man, whose shoulders looked a shade too big for his prison overalls. His untidy brown hair was streaked with gray. His face was sallow but his eyes were sharp.

He was escorted by a burly prison guard.

"Sit down here, please, sir," the guard said. He was firm yet respectful with the dangerous killer.

Prisoner Kane sat. He stared at May. With nothing separating them, not even glass, this felt like a very personal encounter. And his eyes were like chips of steel. His face was stone. Apart from a gleam of curiosity, May didn't get any impression at all that this interview was going to go well.

May desperately wanted him to be ready to answer.

"Morning, Mr. Kane," she said. "I'm - er - I'm May Moore." She didn't want to say Deputy, but also didn't want to say Agent. With the guard in earshot and the warden listening in, her actual status was suddenly very complicated.

Kane rested his hands on the table. The cuffs clinked against the steel. It was a cold sound. As cold as his gaze as he stared at her. She saw a chilly intelligence in his eyes.

"Are you comfortable?" she asked him. "Can we organize anything - I guess maybe coffee isn't possible right now, but water, perhaps? A glass of water?" She glanced anxiously at the guard.

Prisoner Kane stared at her for a moment in impassive silence. And then he did something May really hadn't expected him to do.

He burst out laughing. His face contracted in mirth. The sound resonated around the room, reverberating off the empty walls.

May was thoroughly unnerved. The laugh sounded genuine, but was it a sign that Kane was playing with her?

He continued to laugh, but then his amusement began to fade.

"Look at you, May Moore, asking me if I want water," he said. "Not in seven years has anyone asked me that in this room. And I've had a few lawyers and police badgering me over that time, asking this and that." He narrowed his eyes, but she didn't think his gaze was as quite as hard as it had been.

"No, I don't want water. Thank you. But what do you want?" he asked.

Seeing that things had settled down, the guard who had been standing beside Kane, stepped back and walked out through the security door. He closed it, but May was sure he was standing by, ready to burst in again if needed.

"I'm involved in a difficult case," May said. She realized the fragility of her predicament. This man had a son. She was going to be asking him, basically, to betray his son.

This was huge. It suddenly felt insurmountable, but all she could do was attempt the mountain.

"What case?" he asked.

"There have been a number of bombings. Different people have been targeted. They have been killed, and there have also been collateral killings and injuries. We're hunting for the perpetrator, and based on the evidence, it seems that - it seems that your son Dirk might possibly be involved."

"Why do you say that?" he challenged.

"One of the killings was Sheila, the criminal lawyer who handled your case."

He nodded in silence.

"Another was Mrs. Flannery, the art teacher at his school."

He stared impassively at her.

"Another was the manager of a roadhouse diner, Mrs. Barbara Vining. In another, police from the Sunnybrook precinct were targeted. And the most recent victim was a property rental agent who's now retired, but who previously worked in the area, called Mrs. Jacobs."

"Go on?"

"The killings have been very well researched. Some of the bombs have been set up to detonate via family members. There's a lot of intelligence involved in this crime. A lot of planning. And we do believe that Dirk might be a common factor."

May stared at him anxiously.

She had no idea how he would respond to the insinuation that his son was an even bigger criminal than he was. She feared he wouldn't take it well, and braced herself for whatever might come her way.

"You're asking for a lot," he said. "You're basically asking me to give up my son. That's what you want me to do."

May was panicking inwardly. What would the best response be to this difficult question? A yes might put him off answering. But if she said no, she'd need to give reasons. What reasons could she give?

She had the feeling that Kane was watching her with a hint of evil amusement in his gaze as she struggled to formulate the best reply.

"Look," she said eventually. "If your son is the perpetrator, he's going to get caught. At some stage soon. Without a doubt. He's escalating." Now she was the one to watch him carefully as she spoke. "It's a question of when. How many crimes do you want him accused of by the time he stands in the courtroom and faces up to the jury? If he even gets there, and doesn't get shot and killed in a takedown. Or he could decide to flee the state and continue this elsewhere. It wouldn't help if the FBI is on his trail. He might end up being arrested for committing crimes in a state that still has the death penalty."

May saw Kane's eyes narrow at that. She guessed he was acknowledging the truth of what she said. Feeling as if she'd gained a narrow advantage, she quickly pressed on.

"I can tell you now, Mr. Kane, that if he's innocent you won't be doing him any harm, but if he's guilty, you might as well tell us what you know, so we can arrest him before this entire situation gets any worse."

She could see that this evil and intelligent man was considering the logic of her argument.

For another stomach-wrenching minute, she had no idea whether he would accept it or not. But then Frederick Kane let out a resigned breath.

"I'll tell you, but in return, I want something from you."

"What do you want?" May asked, her heart accelerating all over again. She had no idea whether she'd be able to do him the favor he was asking for.

"Books," he said. "I want a parcel of books. The prison library is useless. I'm all done with trying to find something to read in there."

"I guess I can do that," May said, resolving that if she got the information to take the killer down, she would keep her promise and send him the biggest parcel the prison would allow. "What do you like to read?"

"Fiction. Not romance." He shook his head dismissively. "Anything else. Action. Thrillers. Historical. And not set in Minnesota. I see no reason to read stories set in a state I'll never leave."

Again there was a tinge of regret in his tone.

"I'll do that," May promised.

He nodded. "And in return, I will do my part."

She waited anxiously for him to gather his thoughts.

"This sounds like something Dirk could have done. He was always a headstrong boy. Genius intelligence. But a cold boy. He needed my guidance. That could have set him on the right path. But I didn't guide him. I had my own aims, my own issues, and was preoccupied with those. I did not discipline him. I couldn't control my own anger, never mind deal with my son. So he went rogue. It was something I've always regretted."

"It might not have made a difference, really," May said. She felt a brief and unexpected flare of sympathy for the regret in his tone. As a father, she could understand his sadness, although his criminal actions were still unforgivable in her eyes. But in her experience, people really did choose their own path. She didn't have much experience of murder cases, but she knew a few lesser criminals whose children had chosen to be good, law abiding citizens despite the bad example and their adverse circumstances.

"Thank you," Kane said briefly. "So, why are you here? Yes, my boy could have done it. I acknowledge that. All the individuals involved are people who are connected to our family. He was given detention by the art teacher on the day of the shooting. We were evicted by Mrs. Jacobs, the property manager, a few months before the incident. The diner was opposite the place where I shot two people who I thought deserved it. The Sunnybrook police arrested me after I fled the scene. So yes, all connected. But what can I do?"

"We need to find Dirk," May said, but already, Kane was shaking his head.

"He hasn't visited me in years. Hasn't written, hasn't called. I have no idea where he is."

Kane stared at her, and again, she saw that flash of something in his eyes, a momentary look of concern. "He has emailed, though. That's how he has stayed in touch, with update emails, but they never say much and I don't often get to reply. Recently, though, he sent some strange messages. Now, they are making sense."

"What messages?"

"Three weeks ago, he sent one saying, "One is down Dad, it's started." And then, a week or two ago, I got an email saying, "Two are down and we're rolling." I had no idea what they meant. I haven't been able to check my emails for the past week so there may be others. We have limited access to emails."

This made May absolutely certain that the son was the perpetrator, and that he was updating his dad via these mysterious messages.

"Why is he doing this? What started it?" she asked.

"When this happened, he always said one day he'd be ready to get revenge," Kane said. "The deaths of the people he's killed, they're necessary to get him where he wants to go on this revenge mission. He's been harboring a lot of anger. He needed to vent it. And I agree, he won't stop until he has. If I could stop him, I would, believe me."

May felt a thud of disappointment. She had absolutely banked on the fact the father would know. But perhaps Dirk had deliberately not disclosed his location, knowing that he was going to go ahead with the revenge mission.

"Okay, in that case, here's another question," May tried. "You know your son. And I've told you who he's targeted so far. My question now is this. Who will he target next? Because he's lethal. And he's unstoppable. If we can save anyone, we need to try."

Kane thought for a while, tapping his fingers on the steel surface.

"There are two key figures in the case that I would expect him to want to end with, or work up to. But I can't say which of them he would target first. Perhaps I am totally wrong, and he will target neither. But I do know that those two individuals made him very, very angry."

"Who are they?" May asked.

"One is the judge who handed down the verdict. Judge Zackary. She's a senior judge, very well respected, and must be in her late fifties now."

"And the other?" May asked anxiously.

"The other is a key witness, who spoke up after the shooting. Her testimony swung the verdict, despite Sheila trying hard to provide evidence in mitigation. Her name is Sybil Hardy, and she's the owner of the import-export business across the road from the diner. She was looking out of her window at the time. She is probably around the same age, I think."

May let out a deep breath.

She felt more than grateful to Prisoner Kane for his willingness to help. And both these people sounded like strong potential targets.

May needed to get in touch with her team, immediately. They needed to locate these two women, and get to them as soon as possible, if they were to be saved. But she had no idea which of them the killer would target first.

"Thank you," she said.

She stood up and quickly left the room. The guard unlocked the door as she approached it.

Heading down the corridor, May broke into a run.

CHAPTER TWENTY SEVEN

As soon as she was out of the prison, May got on her phone.

She dialed Owen's number while racing to her car. He picked up on the first ring, sounding stressed.

"May. How did it go? Did you get an address for Dirk? Is he involved?"

"I didn't get an address because his father doesn't know where he's staying. He hasn't been in touch for years, beyond sending emails. But the emails he has sent recently make it clear he's the killer."

"If they couldn't trace the emails he sent with the threats from the cabin, they might not be able to trace these ones either," Owen acknowledged. "Not quickly, anyway. Most likely he's using the dark web like he did when he set up the police killings. The only reason he made a 'mistake' that time was to lure the police to the bomb site. So where does that leave us?"

May climbed into her car.

"His father and I discussed who he might target next."

"That was a good idea," Owen said.

"There are two possible targets. They're both women and probably both a similar age. One is the key witness in the case, Sybil Hardy, and the other is the judge - Judge Zackary. So he could be planning on taking either of these down next. They both played an important role in the case, obviously."

"So we need to get to these two people as soon as we can?" Owen said. "The FBI has given up on questioning William for the moment, as he's started contradicting himself with his versions. So we have lots of manpower available."

"We are going to need it. I guess the judge will be at the courtrooms? Dirk's case was tried at the Willow courthouse."

"That's correct. And Sybil Hardy is a company director who owns a business opposite the roadhouse diner."

"Okay, okay." She could hear that Owen was thinking frantically about the best way forward. "So we need to get to these sites as fast as possible. Explain to these people that they are in danger, and get them out and to safety, while we hunt for this guy. That's the most important thing for now, right?"

"Yes, it is. I am sure he plans to target both. I just don't know who he'll choose first."

"Well, we have to try and cover both bases. So let's see who's closest to what."

She heard the clicking of keys. Owen was pulling up a map.

"It looks like you're closest to the diner. It's on the way back from the prison you've just been to. About twenty minutes away I should think?"

"Okay. So I'll head straight there," May said.

"And I'm closest to the courthouse. Probably half an hour away. I'll go there immediately and I'll call Kerry and ask her to meet me there, and see if the FBI can send a full team to both locations. The more people we have, the better, right?"

"We also need to get the bomb squad to both premises," May suggested. "That might be important."

"Absolutely. The bomb squad," Owen agreed.

He sounded a hundred times calmer than May felt.

"You start driving," he told her. "I'll make plans this side, and then go straight to the courthouse."

"Okay. I'll call you soon." May thought quickly and then added, "Be careful, Owen. Stay safe."

But he'd already disconnected and she felt a strange chill of fear that he hadn't heard her last words. She knew they were both heading into a very dangerous situation. But she'd wanted him to hear her warning.

She started her car, activating the light and the siren, because there wasn't a moment to waste and she would have to speed to this scene.

They needed to get these two women out of harm's way.

May was too late to save the other murdered people; they hadn't had enough information to be able to act. But she wouldn't let that happen to these two. Not now that the potential victims had names and faces. They were known to her, and there was a chance of saving them.

May's stomach clenched with anxiety and she drove with a fierce determination.

She had to stop him. She pressed down on the accelerator, and raced toward the diner, hoping against hope that she wasn't too late.

Ruthlessly, she pushed the negative thoughts and feelings aside and focused on the problem.

The most important thing was to stop him now. To make sure that Judge Zackary and Sybil Hardy were out of his reach and in a place of safety. And that the other occupants of both the buildings could be out of range of the bomb blasts.

You can do it, she urged herself, flicking a glance at her reflection in the rearview mirror. You can find this guy and stop him before he kills again.

May put her foot down, and her focus on the road ahead of her.

She was making good time. Already, she could see the turnoff she needed ahead.

With the siren blaring in her ears, May swung the car off the highway and headed down the town's main street.

Ahead of her was the diner, a quaint, old-fashioned place that must have been a popular destination. Following the blast, it was still closed, and now looked to be getting repaired. There were two pickups parked nearby, and a couple of men were working on the shattered brickwork of the walls.

May glanced suspiciously at the vehicles. She had a feeling the killer might be trying to hide, to blend in with the locals. Perhaps he was posing as a construction worker so as not to draw attention to himself. She didn't trust anything out of place at the moment.

But the diner was not where she needed to go. Instead, May had to head across the road, to the pretty, restored, colonial building with planters outside. It looked to be on two separate levels, with an underground parking.

She stopped outside the building. As she rushed toward the entrance, a terrible thought occurred to her.

What if this killer was going to use the arrival of the police to detonate a bomb? What if, by setting foot in the building, she was ensuring the fate of herself and of Sybil Hardy?

For a moment, May felt a paralyzing fear.

She forced herself to overcome it with calm logic. The killer could surely not have predicted that police would have caught up with him so quickly. He had an ego and believed himself to be streets ahead.

For now, she did not think he would construct such a scenario. She mustn't give him powers he didn't possess, May warned herself. She mustn't let fear allow her to be paranoid.

She pushed the door open and entered the building.

An enormous bang made her jump, and her heart leaped into her throat. But it was only the construction team across the road, unloading a delivery of bricks.

Forcing her shattered nerves into coherence, May headed across the tiled floor to the reception desk.

"I'm Deputy Moore, and I need to speak to Sybil Hardy urgently. It's in connection with a murder case. Is she here?" she asked.

The pleasant-faced, silver-haired receptionist shook her head.

"No. She's not here, Deputy."

"Where is she? It's an emergency. For her own safety, I need to get to her as soon as possible."

The receptionist looked alarmed.

"She's not in the country, ma'am. She's on an overseas vacation in Europe at this time. She left last week, and she's only returning next week."

May considered this information, thinking as fast as she could.

Had the killer known she was away? Probably, yes. He seemed to observe his victims very closely and know their movements. Therefore, she guessed that he would be waiting for her to return.

"Has there been anyone here recently, yesterday or today, who was in the building unaccompanied?" she asked, just to be sure. "Any man, in his twenties, who came in for any reason?"

"No, not in the past two days, definitely not. We've had deliveries but they have been in and out. A crew worked on the feature wall in the boardroom, but that was last week already and there were three of them, all people we've used before. Why? What is this?" she asked anxiously.

"At the moment, there is a low risk that this building might be targeted by the criminal who's been setting bombs," May explained.

The receptionist gasped, looking horrified.

"Please, don't panic. The risk is not high. But just as a safety precaution, everyone who can do so, must leave the building for the next hour or two," May said. "The bomb squad is on their way, and will be checking the premises carefully when they arrive. Once it's cleared, you can go back in."

"I understand. I'll let the managers know, and we'll ask everyone to step outside for a couple of hours."

"Thank you," May said.

She turned and rushed out of the building.

This was a dead end. And that meant Dirk had chosen to target the judge first. Dread filled her as she realized what this would mean. Owen was on his way there. Kerry, too.

May had to get there, as soon as she could, because now she knew, without a doubt, that the next bomb would explode in the courthouse.

CHAPTER TWENTY EIGHT

May sped through the streets of Willow, hurtling toward the courthouse as fast as she could. Glancing down at her phone, she stabbed the buttons, trying yet again to call Owen and Kerry. Their phones were not connecting, and she guessed they'd either turned them off for safety reasons, or else that with the evacuation under way, and the chaos in the area, the networks were jammed.

She told herself over and over that they must be okay, but even so, anxiety closed up her throat and made her palms cold as she sped ever closer to the street where the courthouse was located.

The thought of Owen and Kerry being bombed made her sick with fear.

This was, without a doubt, the final showdown.

She had a momentary vision of the killer, cleverly disguised as a hard working construction worker, or services person. She was sure he'd gotten inside, courthouse or not. May cringed at the thought of it, whipping the car around the final bend.

The man was a monster, and in her mind's eye, she saw a distorted, ugly face, eyes glinting with cold, killing rage. But in reality she knew he was most likely a normal guy, just as his father had appeared to be. He could fit in and pretend to be one of the crowd. He could be any of the people she'd passed on the street.

The courthouse was a pretty building, with a white, elegant exterior, columns and white railings. The thought of it being disfigured by a blast was terrible, but it was the people inside that May was more concerned about. Owen, Kerry, Judge Zackary, and the innocent citizens going about their daily work.

She parked, jumped out of the car, and ran as fast as she could.

As she reached the building, she saw to her relief that evacuation was already under way. People were beginning to file outside in an orderly fashion. That must have taken some persuasion, to stop court proceedings. It was definitely not a quick or easy thing for police to do, without a direct bomb threat having been made.

May felt a wave of relief. This was going to be okay. Everything was going to be okay.

She climbed out of the car and rushed over to the main entrance.

And, as she did, a massive boom came from the building's interior, deep inside.

Smoke shot from the windows. A thundering noise filled the air and the ground shook. May almost fell to her knees from the sheer force of it, but she managed to hold on to her balance.

She watched, appalled, knowing that this was not just an explosion. It was a bomb so powerful it would destroy the entire building.

The window glass shattered outward, and a blade of flame shot from one of the gaps, as the emergency sprinklers burst into life.

Horror-struck, May stood there. She didn't know what to do. She felt paralyzed.

"No," she whispered.

Owen and Kerry were in there. May didn't know what to do, but she had to do something.

Bolting toward the building, she rushed to the entrance, forging her way through the billowing smoke.

As she reached the main doorway, a hand grabbed her arm.

It was Kerry, standing just outside the lobby and clearly managing the evacuation process.

"May! Don't go in there! It's dangerous. There could be other bombs."

"But where's Owen? Where is he? Did he get out?"

Kerry made a face. "That, I'm not sure about. Someone told him about a technician, someone from the electrical department, who'd gone down to the basement and was working there. Owen went down to make sure he knew about the evacuation, and to tell him to leave. But I'm sure he got out okay, May."

May stared at her, appalled.

"But the bomb - the explosion - it seemed to come from underground! What if they wired it in the basement?"

"It's likely they did," Kerry said briskly. "Judge Zackary was due to go out for lunch at this time. That was her habit, what she always did. Court recessed at one, and she would go down to the basement, get into her car, and drive down the road to the coffee shop. She told us this as I was escorting her out. She's safe now. Sheriff Jack has taken her to the police department already so she can be guarded there. But May, we've just got to hope Owen survived. You can't go down there now!"

"Oh, yes, I can," May hissed. She could not believe this worst-case scenario. Her partner, who meant so much to her, had gone down, straight into the killing zone. She had to find him! If he was still alive, if he'd managed to escape the blast, she had to help him out.

"No, you mustn't! May, wait! Are you crazy? I absolutely forbid it! It's too dangerous!"

Kerry tightened her grip on May's arm, but May had not had twenty-nine years of being the baby sister without learning evasion techniques for that particular grasp. She stomped on Kerry's foot, twisted her arm away with a hard wrench, and then she was free.

"Don't you dare follow me!" she shouted to her sister. "Stay here and look after things!"

Gulping in what she knew would be her last breath of fresh air, May raced into the building, pursued by Kerry's desperate shouting. Her heart was hammering. The lobby was filled with smoke. She heard discordant clashes as structures began to collapse.

Where were the stairs down? She had to get there!

The building was in complete chaos. Smoke hung in the air. Emergency lights flashed on the walls.

The explosion had destroyed one whole wing of the building, and now it was blazing.

Spotting a stairwell, she raced to it as fast as she could.

May charged down the stairs, two at a time. The smoke was thicker down here, and she got to the bottom and almost choked.

"Owen!" she screamed.

The basement was ruined. The explosion had flung debris everywhere, and smoke seethed through the underground space. She could see the shells of cars, some on their sides, that looked to have been damaged and destroyed in the blast.

She could hear the fire crackling and growing to her right, as it ate up more and more of the building.

Was he here? She had to find him. She needed to find him!

May didn't know where to even begin. He could be anywhere, he could be hurt and dying, and she wouldn't know.

"Owen!" May screamed, her voice tearing her throat. Why wasn't he answering? Was he even still down here, or was he dead, and she'd gotten here too late?

Half running, half falling over the debris, swerving to avoid an overturned car, she lunged ahead. She was desperately trying to control her breathing to spare her from inhaling too much smoke.

She jumped as, from the far side of the basement, another minor blast rang out and the whole structure shook. Plaster fell from above and a pillar quivered.

That was a car, May thought. That had been a car exploding. Perhaps a second lot of explosives had been in another car, or else the gas tank had gone up.

She didn't know. All she knew was that she hadn't found Owen.

She ran on, stumbling over the rubble, getting closer to the burning chaos that she knew represented the epicenter of the explosion. She was so terrified of losing him, that she forgot to be afraid of the whole building coming down on top of her.

And then, she saw it.

Slumped behind a pillar. A body, on the ground. But in the flickering light from a nearby fire, she recognized the shape of the jaw, the form of the haircut.

It was Owen lying there. Without a doubt.

"No!" May shouted, her voice now hysterical.

She rushed forward, praying that by a miracle he'd survived the blast, but knowing deep inside that she might have to accept the worst.

CHAPTER TWENTY NINE

"Owen! Owen!" May yelled.

Her deputy was lying on the ground, his eyes closed, his body still. She fell to her knees by his side and felt for a pulse on his outstretched hand.

Through the billowing smoke, she noticed that he was wearing his bulletproof vest, and that he'd fallen behind one of the metal supports in the basement.

Had that been enough to save him, to ensure his survival?

Her fingers were trembling, but she found the pulse. He was alive!

"Owen! Owen, can you hear me?

Owen groaned. His hand twitched, and then his eyes opened.

"Wow, that was some blast," he said in a hoarse voice, and then coughed. He sat up gingerly, blinking.

"We need to get out of here, May. It looks like this whole place is about to burn down."

Relief flooded through her. Owen was okay. She knew he would need to be thoroughly checked out by the medics, but the fact that he was able to move, and to speak, and that he knew where he was and what had happened, indicated that no serious harm had been done and he was simply stunned by the force of the blast.

"Yes, we need to get out. As fast as we can." She helped him to his feet.

There was no way of knowing how much time they had before the whole place burned down, and they both knew it. The fire was growing ever fiercer and it felt as if the building was about to collapse under the weight of the blaze.

She stumbled with him over the rubble, making for the stairs. May hoped that they would still be able to get up that way.

"I hope it's still clear enough to get up here. The fire was quite bad," she gasped, coughing.

"There's another way," Owen choked out. "I can go and see if it's still passable. It might be blocked."

"We need two choices. The stairs might collapse."

"I'll go see if the other door is open. It's not far away. I'll be a minute, and I'll come back and find you. If your way is open, we go out. Otherwise, we go back the other direction. We meet here, right? Here. Near this overturned Lexus. In one minute's time."

They both turned around, taking in their surroundings, knowing that they could change within a minute if the smoke thickened, but that this was the best course of action.

Then Owen hurried off, and May forged forward, hoping that the stairs were still clear, and they could get up that way.

Then she saw a figure approaching her through the smoke. Her heart lifted, because surely that meant they had just come down the stairs? Was it a fireman or a policeman, coming down to locate them?

But then, she thought again.

Because this figure was tall and rangy, and clutching something in his hand. He had a backpack slung over his shoulder and he was wearing an electrical company's overalls, and he was approaching her with intent. This was not a first responder. There was no police uniform, no reflective clothing, no Kevlar, no helmet. And no signs of panic. He wasn't an innocent electrician trying to escape. He was confronting her.

It was the killer. It had to be. He was disguised as an electrician and that was how he'd gotten down here to plant the bombs. What irony that Owen had gone down to rescue him! And now, he was here, on site, watching May blunder through his death zone.

"Well, here you are! Are you one of the police who's been chasing me?" he said, his voice hoarse. "What have you done with the judge? Judge Zackary! Where is she? Did you take her out of the courthouse? The video played! The bomb exploded! And she wasn't there!"

Now his voice was cracking with fury. May had never heard such maddened rage.

May's hand instinctively dropped to her gun. She needed to take this guy out, immediately.

But he gave her a warning shake of the head.

"Oh, no. You don't do that. Because if I see your hand move, then I'm going to pull the fuse that detonates this baby. If I do that, we both die. This is a very powerful bomb," he told her, coughing slightly as he spoke. "And I need to use it. I didn't get to use it on my target. You prevented that, despite all my planning. You made things go wrong. That's unforgivable. Nothing was supposed to go wrong! Call the judge. Get her back here. I want Judge Zackary. Bring her to me!"

His eyes were glittering. May sensed that this man had crossed a line into madness.

"I can't do that. She's already in a safe place. And please, don't detonate the bomb," she said. "We'll both die if you do."

He laughed, but there was no humor in it. "You don't know me at all, but I'll share a personal fact with you. I don't listen to what people like you say. I never have and I never will. I'm a rebel. But now, thanks to you, I'm an angry rebel, who had a failure."

"You're a terrorist," May retorted.

"Don't flatter me, lady cop. The term 'terrorist' is so overused these days, but yes, I suppose you could call me that. I'm an activist and I believe that violence is the only way to get the results I need for my personal mission, and I am prepared to bring the full force of that violence down on those who oppose me. And those who prevent me from achieving my goals," he added threateningly.

She kept her hand still at her side, knowing if she made a move, he would see. She didn't even dare to twitch her fingers. She was pretty sure that he would follow through on his threats, and it would be the end.

A car behind them exploded. The blast reverberated through the basement and they both jumped. May felt an immediate pang of anxiety for Owen. Had he been near that car? Where was the other exit point he was hoping to find?

Would he get out okay?

She was terrified that he'd come back to find her and that his arrival would trigger the killer. This entire situation was teetering on a knife-edge of possibilities, none of them good.

"I only just got here. I don't even know much about you," she tried. Perhaps if she could get him talking, he might be less trigger-happy about the bomb. "Why are you doing this?"

"My problem is with society as a whole. It's corrupt. People do what they want. And innocent people get caught up in it. I just set the balance right. But I've got a lot more to do. I have many more targets in my sight. I'm nowhere near done yet. I've almost completed my personal hit list, but then I'm going to move on. You have no clue what an exciting time I have planned. But anyway, all this is the reason I can't let you stop me. The reason you have to let me walk away, or you die. And then I die too. So, if I were you, I'd just close my eyes. When you open them, I'll be gone."

May felt a chill. This man had her trapped. She couldn't use her gun or she would die. He was willing to let them both die if he had to, but otherwise he was coercing her to look away so he could escape. And if she did that, then he would carry on with his deadly mission.

Could she possibly distract him enough to get to her gun? It was her only hope right now. He was egotistical, that she saw. If he kept talking, perhaps he'd get carried away with his diatribe and forget about the explosion.

"So, you're going to keep killing to get your message out?"

"You're right. You're absolutely correct."

"Do you think you're more intelligent than most of society?" May asked, pandering to that monster ego she sensed.

"Of course I am. People are stupid and blind."

"So you're opening their eyes?"

"Exactly. I've ignited a fire, a big fire. I've lit a fuse that is going to cause a lot of people to pay attention to the injustices of society. I'm going to get people to consider how things could be done differently."

"Couldn't you do it differently?" she quizzed.

"How else would I get the message out?" he replied disparagingly.

Her talking hadn't worked so far. His hand was still tight on the bomb. He wasn't relaxing the way she needed him to.

May knew she had very little time left. The building was collapsing around them. The blaze was getting closer. In a matter of moments, they would both be trapped here.

She would die, and May had to force herself to accept this terrible reality. She would just have to try and be brave.

Smoke was swirling closer, reminding her of a figure, creeping in the shadows.

Only then, May saw that it actually was a figure, creeping in the shadows. It was Owen. He was sidling from behind the ruined car, creeping to the pillar a few yards to the left of Dirk. He must have arrived back and overheard her dialogue with the killer.

Now, he was maneuvering around, trying to get behind him. She dared to allow herself the faintest breath of hope. If he managed to surprise him from behind, Dirk might just let go of that bomb. She didn't think Owen would risk a shot, knowing that if he didn't kill Dirk outright then he would still be able to detonate the bomb. She thought he was going to go for a physical tackle, to grab his arms. Or maybe grasp his throat, to cause him to reflexively let go of that device.

May had never thought she'd be in such a risky situation in her entire life, and now, the pressure was on her. Now, she had to keep Dirk's focus on her, or he might see Owen and then it would all be over.

"What would your father say if he saw you now?" she asked.

The question startled him. He stared at her in shock.

"My father?" he said, his eyes narrowing. "How do you know about my father?"

"I spoke to him today. I went and asked him about you. That's how we know who you are, Dirk," May said firmly.

She saw his face contort in anger.

"You did that? How dare you do that! You have no right to go to my family behind my back!"

"In the course of the investigation, I spoke to him," May said. "But that's not the point. Would he be proud of what you're doing? Would he approve?"

She knew she was playing with fire, and that she was close to dying. But she needed to keep this man talking, while Owen got closer.

The man laughed, but it was a humorless, brittle sound, and she could tell he was still angry.

"He would if he saw the results of it. He was a big believer in revenge. Maybe he's gotten softer in jail, but he was, for sure."

"Tell me, why did you target the art teacher?" she asked. "I mean, why art?"

Now, Owen was directly behind Dirk, about ten feet away.

Dirk was clearly surprised that May had asked him this question.

"She kept me in detention at the wrong time. Sometimes, it's only the timing that matters."

His head jerked to the right as a pillar collapsed.

"But she was just an innocent teacher," May tried.

Owen was prowling closer. She had to keep Dirk's attention.

"I already told you!"

"And the cops? How did you send those emails?"

"Because I know how to use the dark web, and I went looking for an unoccupied cabin so I could set someone else up as the suspect, and trap the cops."

"That's interesting," May said.

To her amazement, she saw she'd managed to buy enough time to allow Owen to make his attack.

He'd gotten close, and now, May realized, the most dangerous part of this entire encounter was about to play out.

If Owen didn't get that bomb out of Dirk's hand, then without a doubt, they would all die.

If he managed, then they were still in huge danger, but they had a chance.

She held her breath as, behind the bomber, Owen made his charge, rushing at the man with all the speed he possessed.

135

CHAPTER THIRTY

May braced herself, ready for the worst, but prepared to do whatever she could to disarm the killer and get his bomb away from him.

Owen landed on the man's shoulders and she watched Dirk's face contort in utter shock. He wrenched at Dirk's arms, and she saw his grasp slip. Grabbing him from behind had been totally unexpected, and he hadn't been braced against it.

This was her chance.

May rushed forward and grabbed hold of the bomb, her heart hammering as she tugged it away from him. She was no bomb squad expert. She had no idea what might detonate this terrifying and surprisingly heavy device. Was the fuse attached to Dirk? It hadn't sounded like it from what he'd said, but it could be that he'd done that.

She had no choice but to take its full weight in her hands, because Owen was on the attack, preventing Dirk from getting hold of it again.

Owen clamped his hands on either side of the man's neck and squeezed, his fingers digging into the flesh of his victim's throat. Dirk began screaming and thrashing, trying to throw Owen off.

And May staggered back, now the new owner of this deadly bomb.

She crept a few paces away and set it down carefully. She didn't trust it, not one bit. It might still detonate. And he could have planted other bombs. For now, this basement was a high risk area.

Seeing a blinking light on the side of the bomb, May stared down in horror, realizing the impossible truth as she took in the information on the screen.

It was a countdown device.

The bomb must have a manual override system that Dirk had threatened her with. But otherwise, May saw to her horror, it was due to activate in exactly two minutes.

No wonder Dirk had been laughing so confidently, so maniacally. She guessed that at the last minute, he'd planned to throw the bomb in her direction and race away to the stairs. He'd been watching the timer, planning. No wonder he'd been happy to keep talking. It had suited him, too.

Two minutes was all they had to get out. She didn't know if they could do it.

Then, hearing a grunt and a cry from behind, she spun around, her hand dropping instinctively to her gun. Despairingly, May saw things were not going well. In fact, the fight had changed course completely.

Dirk was on the attack. He'd thrown himself backward, knocking Owen off balance, and had wriggled out of his grasp. Now the two men were wrestling on the ground. She heard grunts and cries, and the thud of fists making contact with flesh.

In the thick, billowing smoke, as they fought and rolled, May didn't dare to use her gun. It was too risky.

Instead, she rushed forward to join the fray. They had to try and subdue this man, but he was fighting like a demon.

Dirk was far stronger than she'd guessed him to be, and he was clearly powered by desperation and fury. He was using his fists and his feet, and he had not given up.

May charged forward, adrenaline surging. Two minutes was all they had before a lethal explosion that annihilated them all.

She heard his fist connect with Owen's gut, and she saw her deputy go down. Dirk raised his hand and punched him hard in the throat. Owen convulsed, choking desperately.

And then, Dirk burst free, throwing himself at May. Grabbing her arm, he flung her directly back into Owen.

He was going for the bomb.

May made one desperate grab for him, knowing that it was all she had time for in this life or death situation.

By a miracle, in the smoky semi-dark, she managed to catch hold of one of his legs. She sprawled on the concrete floor, grasping it with all her might, trying to hold him back from reaching that lethal weapon. Never had it been more important to keep her grip. But then, his other boot came up and caught her in the face - a painful, head-snapping blow.

She recoiled back, her cheek on fire. She felt her grasp on his boot slipping and her stomach tensed as he jerked free.

But Owen was on his feet now, racing forward, grabbing Dirk's arm and jerking him away.

Snarling, Dirk twisted around, throwing a vicious punch that Owen only just managed to avoid. But he was ready to retaliate, even though he was badly off balance.

She saw Owen's fist connect his solar plexus, and now Dirk was the one off balance.

He reeled back, his breath escaping him, and May turned the moment into a full-on tackle.

She rushed at Dirk, aiming a kick for his stomach, then aiming an uppercut for his chin. May wasn't a fighter, but she was desperate, and she realized she might be able to buy them some time, if she could just get in a few good blows.

Dirk was quick, though. He dodged her third blow, and with a powerful swing of his arm, he slammed her in the chest with a side-arm swipe that made her gasp and stagger back. May fell down onto one hand, landing painfully on a sharp chunk of stone.

But Owen had attacked again from behind, and putting his full weight into the tackle, Owen slammed Dirk onto the ground. He kicked out at his head, getting in a solid blow, and Dirk's neck snapped back.

Finally, he sprawled to the ground, seeming dazed. The vicious intent went out of his eyes, and they dulled. His head slumped back. Temporarily at least, he was down and out, and that gave them a sliver of a chance.

"We don't have any more time, Owen! We have to get out of here!" May cried, pointing to the escape route she'd tried to find earlier. "The bomb was set on two minutes. We have less than one minute left!"

But as she said the words, one of the concrete pillars nearby finally gave way, and the ceiling began to collapse.

With a roar, the area to the right of them gave way, plummeting down with a crash. That was the way they needed to go! And now it was blocked.

May tried to breathe, but she couldn't. The air was full of dust, smoke, and concrete. She coughed, her throat aching. Her eyes were burning.

She couldn't see Owen, but she heard him coughing too.

"Owen!" she tried yelling. "Owen!"

In the dusty madness, his hand grabbed hers.

"Come the other way," he yelled. "The route this side was open!"

May raced alongside him, clumsy and stumbling in the darkness that was littered with debris. Behind them, they heard the roaring crash of another pillar collapsing. Ahead, the burning hulk of a car blocked their way and they veered around it, with May hoping the gas tank wouldn't choose that moment to blow.

It was a neck and neck race as to which would happen first - the total collapse of the basement, or the devastating bomb blast behind them.

And they had to fight through a lethal obstacle course to find the other exit point - wherever it was. She hoped Owen would remember the way in this chaos, because May now had no idea where they were.

They raced through the maze of debris and dust, tripping and slipping over the rubble, dodging around cars. They were moving as fast as they could through an unplanned obstacle course. May was sure they had only a few seconds left before that bomb detonated.

She kept running, hearing the sounds of the concrete smashing and raining down all around her. A chunk of brick hit her a painful blow on the shoulder and she staggered.

And then, ahead, she saw a faint light - a beam of hope in the darkness. The fire exit door.

"There!" she cried, pointing. "There, Owen!"

Racing toward the door, May flung her shoulder against it, feeling it give way.

They'd made it!

And then, just as they burst out of the door and into the open air, she heard the explosion behind them. The roaring, tearing blast sounded like a thousand trucks crashing into each other.

She was thrown out, the force of the blast tossing her away from the door and across the paved yard. She felt herself flying, and then hitting the ground with a hard, painful thump. The air was forced out of her lungs. Her head cracked down, and she crumpled.

She lay there, her limbs weak. Pain blossomed in her head, her chest, her arms, and her back. Her ears were ringing.

She opened her eyes. They were streaming and burning. In the distance, ambulance sirens were getting louder.

Owen was beside her, prone, but breathing.

They'd gotten out. Against all the odds, they had made it to safety before the final blast.

And, as the basement finally collapsed with a terrible, cracking sound, May knew for sure that it was the killer's final refuge.

Dirk had taken his last stand in there, been trapped, and had died among the destruction he'd caused.

At last, they had caught the killer, and it seemed only fitting that he had been the final victim in the lethal scenario he'd engineered. The man who had caused so much terror and death had been unable to escape his final bomb blast, and now, at last, the nightmare was over.

140

CHAPTER THIRTY ONE

The hospital bed was comfortable, clean, and above all, it was free from smoke, rubble, or anything resembling a bomb blast, May thought appreciatively.

She had been taken straight from the bombed-out courtroom to the local Willow hospital. Kerry had insisted on riding with her, and had held her hand the whole way in the ambulance. It had been an exhausting, though strangely uplifting ride. Her sister had alternated between hysterical tears of relief, and hoarse-voiced promises that she was going to get May back for not listening to her, as soon as she'd been checked out and they knew nothing was wrong.

Once in the hospital, she was admitted as a day patient, while she got treated for smoke inhalation, had three cuts stitched, and a few X-rays taken. Owen had also been admitted and was receiving the same treatment.

The nurse who'd brought her tea and snacks a few minutes earlier, bustled into the room again. This time, she was carrying two large arrangements of flowers.

May stared at them in surprise.

"One is from Judge Zackary, and one is from students at the local Willow school," the nurse explained. "There are a few more down in reception. I've taken two others through to Deputy Owen Lovell, also."

She stared at May and then asked, "Would you mind - I know it's not professional of me, but my daughter has been following this case. She's just started work at the business across the street from the roadhouse diner, and has been so anxious. She asked if I could take a selfie with you?"

May knew she didn't look her best at all. Her hair was still covered in dust and grime, and she had a dressing on one side of her face. But she guessed that was the point. A selfie straight from a battle scene would definitely make the daughter happy.

"Sure," she said.

"Oh, thank you!" The nurse moved forward, got out her phone, and quickly snapped the shot.

A moment later, there was a tap on the door.

May looked around, astonished to see her parents advancing into the room. Her mother was carrying a large box of chocolates, and a container of fruit juice.

"May!" her mother said. "I just couldn't believe it when I heard that you went into the courthouse, into certain danger, to save your deputy, and that you and your deputy fought off that killer in a collapsing basement? Is it true?"

May nodded. "Yes, Mom. It's true."

"Well, all I can say is that it's the most incredible bravery. I am so proud that you're my daughter! Aren't we both proud?" she asked May's father.

"We sure are," he said. "On the way in, we met Kerry's boss, Agent Keith Ross. They are about to board a helicopter to fly back, but he came here first to give you his personal congratulations. As soon as we leave, he'll be on his way in."

"What?" May asked, incredulously. The FBI big boss wanted to thank her personally? Was she dreaming?

But she couldn't be, as her mother continued. "He was also saying that this was the most incredible takedown. That if the killer had managed to escape, he would definitely have set more bombs and killed more people. He sounded so admiring of you!"

"Thank you," May said.

She felt warm inside. She simply couldn't believe that they had managed to do this, against such adverse odds and in such danger.

And she felt relieved beyond words that Owen was okay. She still remembered the way she'd felt when she had thought he was dead.

That moment, that knowledge, had clenched at her heart in a way she didn't want to think about. It had felt like the worst experience of her entire life.

It had felt more intense than it should have if it had been her investigation partner lying there, even though they worked together so closely. She'd felt more emotional than that.

May acknowledged that. Now, she knew that she had not been honest with herself, about her own feelings, when she'd said she did not want to date him.

The feelings were there. She had to confront that truth. Now, it would be up to her whether she kept denying them or not.

The thought made her feel all kinds of things - nervous, worried, excited, and a little puzzled.

But above all, she realized that she felt hopeful.

"I am sure you need to recover and have a quiet evening at home tonight," her mother said. "But tomorrow, you must come around for dinner. And perhaps you'd like to invite your deputy? It would be wonderful to meet him, since you saved each other's lives. Do you think he'd enjoy a home cooked meal with us as a thank-you?"

"I think he'd love it," May said.

"Well, then. I'm thinking of doing a roast beef, with roast potatoes, gravy, and all the trimmings. I will go and shop for the ingredients now. We can't take up too much of your time now, sweetheart."

"Not with the FBI waiting to congratulate you," her father emphasized, raising his eyebrows conspiratorially. "Well done, May. I could not be prouder."

They turned and left, leaving May floating on a happy cloud.

And then, the door opened and FBI Senior Special Agent Keith Ross walked in, with Sheriff Jack beside him.

Sheriff Jack gave her a quick grin and a proud nod as the FBI senior executive walked up to her hospital bed.

"Well done, May," he said quietly as she gave him a grin in return, before turning her focus to the FBI exec.

"Deputy Moore, I hope you are feeling better after your ordeal," Agent Ross said.

"I'm fine, thank you, sir" she replied. "Luckily, just minor injuries."

"I wanted to tell you, personally, how impressed I am with you," he said. "Agent Kerry Moore explained to me the thought processes you used to identify the killer, and the steps you took - obviously, I had to be urgently briefed, as I called the prison to get you the interview."

"Thank you for that," May said. "It was very helpful."

"You are the one who should be thanked, for the line of logic that led you there and allowed the police and FBI to save many lives today." He paused. "The way you took on that killer and saved your deputy personifies the kind of capability and bravery that we seek, and applaud, in the FBI. You are a credit to your police department and you should be very proud of what you achieved today."

"Thank you," she said, feeling breathless at the praise.

"I know your superiors will take special note of your excellent work. I will follow up on the investigation personally, and I'm sure that your dedication will be recognized." He smiled at her. "Now, I have to be on my way back to the Virginia head office for a meeting. I hope we'll see each other again soon."

They turned and left the room. The FBI agent peeled off left, clearly heading for the exit, but May was pleased to see that Sheriff

Jack turned right. She knew her boss was going straight to Owen's ward, to give him the congratulations and commendations that he deserved.

What an outcome.

May still couldn't believe the events of the past thirty-six hours. She felt as if a whirlwind had come and gone, a tornado that should have caused destruction, but that somehow, had managed to leave her with a sense of motivation and hope.

At least the deaths of the innocent victims had been avenged and their families now had closure, and further deaths had been prevented.

But as she thought back to the rubble and devastation that had littered the building, it gave May a glimpse of insight into another, different challenge she was facing.

Suddenly she had an idea of where that watcher might have been standing on the day that Lauren disappeared.

Tomorrow evening, when she went to her parents for dinner, May decided she would detour there on the way and see if her theory was correct.

EPILOGUE

It was a beautiful, sunny evening as May approached the place, two streets down from her parents' house, which she now thought must be where the person filming Lauren had stood.

She had traveled straight here from the post office, where she'd sent Prisoner Kane a delivery of twenty brand new novels. She had kept her side of the bargain. And even a hardened criminal was going to feel sorrow and guilt on the loss of a son. May hoped the books would provide a distraction to him at this time.

After sending the books, May now had ten minutes to figure out if her theory about the video threat was right. After that, she would have to hustle for dinner with her parents. She didn't want to be late, and wanted to arrive early, since Owen had been invited, too.

But for now, with the setting sun sinking below the tree line, she climbed out of her car and made her way over to the location.

It was the abandoned mill. A small plot of ground that had once housed the local mill, but which had since fallen into disuse. It was a historic site, which people came to view, despite the fact that the stone walls had largely collapsed.

But she was sure this was where Lauren's captor had stood. The reason the video had been so blurry was that it was so far away, and had been on the maximum zoom setting. There was a heap of stones that she thought might replicate the exact angle she'd seen, if Lauren's captor had stood on it.

May walked over to the stones, feeling her spine prickle.

Carefully, she clambered up and stood there.

From here, she could see her parents' front door clearly. She could almost smell the rich scents of cooking that she knew were filling the house. Lights were on in the windows. Everything would be perfect, for this dinner in honor of May and Owen.

But here, ten years ago, someone had lurked with evil intent watching that same door.

May stepped down from the stones. In front of them was a pile of loose gravel. Wondering suddenly if it might still hold a clue, a trace of some residual evidence, she rummaged through the gravel, feeling curious, moving the sharp stones aside. Could this person have dropped something? Anything? A lens cap, a credit card, a ring?

It was highly unlikely, and probably a waste of time even to try. But she found it impossible to stop as she sifted through the gravel, curiosity filling her.

And then, May's fingers touched something smooth and small, and she picked it up, holding it between her index finger and thumb.

Her eyes widened as she saw what it was.

She couldn't believe it. What did this mean? What could it mean?

In her hand, she was holding an old, slightly rusted key.

It was uncannily similar to the one May had found in the evidence box. It looked to be the same age, the same type of steel and the same model, but this one had a much longer shaft.

The keys must somehow be linked, May thought, and that surely gave her much more of a lead to their purpose. Did they open the same container? Were they both from the same house or building?

May was even more convinced now that these keys had to hold the answer to Lauren's disappearance.

Gripping it tightly in her hand, she turned away and headed back to her car, feeling breathless with shock and surprise, but even more determined to pursue this cold case with all the resources she had.

She was going to find out where these keys led and what they unlocked.

May felt sure that the secret to her sister's disappearance would be waiting behind that door.

NOW AVAILABLE!

NEVER AGAIN
(A May Moore Suspense Thriller—Book 6)

From #1 bestselling mystery and suspense author Blake Pierce comes a gripping new series: May Moore, 29, an average Midwestern woman and deputy sheriff, has always lived in the shadow of her older, brilliant FBI agent sister. Yet the sisters are united by the cold case of their missing younger sister—and when a new serial killer strikes in May's quiet, Minnesota lakeside town, it is May's turn to prove herself, to try to outshine her sister and the FBI, and, in this action-packed thriller, to outwit and hunt down a diabolical killer before he strikes again.

"A masterpiece of thriller and mystery."
—Books and Movie Reviews, Roberto Mattos (re Once Gone)

After a local manhunt for a missing woman, a pack of cadaver dogs lead police to the source.

But when the dogs unearth body after body, May soon realizes she has stumbled upon a burial mound—and is up against a serial killer for more deadly than anyone could have imagined.

With time running out, can May find him—before he finds her first?

A page-turning and harrowing crime thriller featuring a brilliant and tortured Deputy Sheriff, the MAY MOORE series is a riveting mystery, packed with non-stop action, suspense, jaw-dropping twists, and driven by a breakneck pace that will keep you flipping pages late into the night.

Future books in the series will be available soon!

"An edge of your seat thriller in a new series that keeps you turning pages! ...So many twists, turns and red herrings... I can't wait to see what happens next."
—Reader review (Her Last Wish)

"A strong, complex story about two FBI agents trying to stop a serial killer. If you want an author to capture your attention and have you guessing, yet trying to put the pieces together, Pierce is your author!"
—Reader review (Her Last Wish)

"A typical Blake Pierce twisting, turning, roller coaster ride suspense thriller. Will have you turning the pages to the last sentence of the last chapter!!!"
—Reader review (City of Prey)

"Right from the start we have an unusual protagonist that I haven't seen done in this genre before. The action is nonstop... A very atmospheric novel that will keep you turning pages well into the wee hours."
—Reader review (City of Prey)

"Everything that I look for in a book... a great plot, interesting characters, and grabs your interest right away. The book moves along at a breakneck pace and stays that way until the end. Now on go I to book two!"
—Reader review (Girl, Alone)

"Exciting, heart pounding, edge of your seat book... a must read for mystery and suspense readers!"
—Reader review (Girl, Alone)

Blake Pierce

Blake Pierce is the USA Today bestselling author of the RILEY PAGE mystery series, which includes seventeen books. Blake Pierce is also the author of the MACKENZIE WHITE mystery series, comprising fourteen books; of the AVERY BLACK mystery series, comprising six books; of the KERI LOCKE mystery series, comprising five books; of the MAKING OF RILEY PAIGE mystery series, comprising six books; of the KATE WISE mystery series, comprising seven books; of the CHLOE FINE psychological suspense mystery, comprising six books; of the JESSE HUNT psychological suspense thriller series, comprising twenty four books; of the AU PAIR psychological suspense thriller series, comprising three books; of the ZOE PRIME mystery series, comprising six books; of the ADELE SHARP mystery series, comprising sixteen books, of the EUROPEAN VOYAGE cozy mystery series, comprising four books; of the new LAURA FROST FBI suspense thriller, comprising nine books (and counting); of the new ELLA DARK FBI suspense thriller, comprising eleven books (and counting); of the A YEAR IN EUROPE cozy mystery series, comprising nine books, of the AVA GOLD mystery series, comprising six books (and counting); of the RACHEL GIFT mystery series, comprising eight books (and counting); of the VALERIE LAW mystery series, comprising nine books (and counting); of the PAIGE KING mystery series, comprising six books (and counting); of the MAY MOORE mystery series, comprising six books (and counting); and the CORA SHIELDS mystery series, comprising three books (and counting).

An avid reader and lifelong fan of the mystery and thriller genres, Blake loves to hear from you, so please feel free to visit www.blakepierceauthor.com to learn more and stay in touch.

BOOKS BY BLAKE PIERCE

CORA SHIELDS MYSTERY SERIES
UNDONE (Book #1)
UNWANTED (Book #2)
UNHINGED (Book #3)

MAY MOORE SUSPENSE THRILLER
NEVER RUN (Book #1)
NEVER TELL (Book #2)
NEVER LIVE (Book #3)
NEVER HIDE (Book #4)
NEVER FORGIVE (Book #5)
NEVER AGAIN (Book #6)

PAIGE KING MYSTERY SERIES
THE GIRL HE PINED (Book #1)
THE GIRL HE CHOSE (Book #2)
THE GIRL HE TOOK (Book #3)
THE GIRL HE WISHED (Book #4)
THE GIRL HE CROWNED (Book #5)
THE GIRL HE WATCHED (Book #6)

VALERIE LAW MYSTERY SERIES
NO MERCY (Book #1)
NO PITY (Book #2)
NO FEAR (Book #3)
NO SLEEP (Book #4)
NO QUARTER (Book #5)
NO CHANCE (Book #6)
NO REFUGE (Book #7)
NO GRACE (Book #8)
NO ESCAPE (Book #9)

RACHEL GIFT MYSTERY SERIES
HER LAST WISH (Book #1)
HER LAST CHANCE (Book #2)

HER LAST HOPE (Book #3)
HER LAST FEAR (Book #4)
HER LAST CHOICE (Book #5)
HER LAST BREATH (Book #6)
HER LAST MISTAKE (Book #7)
HER LAST DESIRE (Book #8)

AVA GOLD MYSTERY SERIES
CITY OF PREY (Book #1)
CITY OF FEAR (Book #2)
CITY OF BONES (Book #3)
CITY OF GHOSTS (Book #4)
CITY OF DEATH (Book #5)
CITY OF VICE (Book #6)

A YEAR IN EUROPE
A MURDER IN PARIS (Book #1)
DEATH IN FLORENCE (Book #2)
VENGEANCE IN VIENNA (Book #3)
A FATALITY IN SPAIN (Book #4)

ELLA DARK FBI SUSPENSE THRILLER
GIRL, ALONE (Book #1)
GIRL, TAKEN (Book #2)
GIRL, HUNTED (Book #3)
GIRL, SILENCED (Book #4)
GIRL, VANISHED (Book 5)
GIRL ERASED (Book #6)
GIRL, FORSAKEN (Book #7)
GIRL, TRAPPED (Book #8)
GIRL, EXPENDABLE (Book #9)
GIRL, ESCAPED (Book #10)
GIRL, HIS (Book #11)

LAURA FROST FBI SUSPENSE THRILLER
ALREADY GONE (Book #1)
ALREADY SEEN (Book #2)
ALREADY TRAPPED (Book #3)
ALREADY MISSING (Book #4)
ALREADY DEAD (Book #5)

ALREADY TAKEN (Book #6)
ALREADY CHOSEN (Book #7)
ALREADY LOST (Book #8)
ALREADY HIS (Book #9)

EUROPEAN VOYAGE COZY MYSTERY SERIES
MURDER (AND BAKLAVA) (Book #1)
DEATH (AND APPLE STRUDEL) (Book #2)
CRIME (AND LAGER) (Book #3)
MISFORTUNE (AND GOUDA) (Book #4)
CALAMITY (AND A DANISH) (Book #5)
MAYHEM (AND HERRING) (Book #6)

ADELE SHARP MYSTERY SERIES
LEFT TO DIE (Book #1)
LEFT TO RUN (Book #2)
LEFT TO HIDE (Book #3)
LEFT TO KILL (Book #4)
LEFT TO MURDER (Book #5)
LEFT TO ENVY (Book #6)
LEFT TO LAPSE (Book #7)
LEFT TO VANISH (Book #8)
LEFT TO HUNT (Book #9)
LEFT TO FEAR (Book #10)
LEFT TO PREY (Book #11)
LEFT TO LURE (Book #12)
LEFT TO CRAVE (Book #13)
LEFT TO LOATHE (Book #14)
LEFT TO HARM (Book #15)
LEFT TO RUIN (Book #16)

THE AU PAIR SERIES
ALMOST GONE (Book#1)
ALMOST LOST (Book #2)
ALMOST DEAD (Book #3)

ZOE PRIME MYSTERY SERIES
FACE OF DEATH (Book#1)
FACE OF MURDER (Book #2)
FACE OF FEAR (Book #3)

FACE OF MADNESS (Book #4)
FACE OF FURY (Book #5)
FACE OF DARKNESS (Book #6)

A JESSIE HUNT PSYCHOLOGICAL SUSPENSE SERIES
THE PERFECT WIFE (Book #1)
THE PERFECT BLOCK (Book #2)
THE PERFECT HOUSE (Book #3)
THE PERFECT SMILE (Book #4)
THE PERFECT LIE (Book #5)
THE PERFECT LOOK (Book #6)
THE PERFECT AFFAIR (Book #7)
THE PERFECT ALIBI (Book #8)
THE PERFECT NEIGHBOR (Book #9)
THE PERFECT DISGUISE (Book #10)
THE PERFECT SECRET (Book #11)
THE PERFECT FAÇADE (Book #12)
THE PERFECT IMPRESSION (Book #13)
THE PERFECT DECEIT (Book #14)
THE PERFECT MISTRESS (Book #15)
THE PERFECT IMAGE (Book #16)
THE PERFECT VEIL (Book #17)
THE PERFECT INDISCRETION (Book #18)
THE PERFECT RUMOR (Book #19)
THE PERFECT COUPLE (Book #20)
THE PERFECT MURDER (Book #21)
THE PERFECT HUSBAND (Book #22)
THE PERFECT SCANDAL (Book #23)
THE PERFECT MASK (Book #24)

CHLOE FINE PSYCHOLOGICAL SUSPENSE SERIES
NEXT DOOR (Book #1)
A NEIGHBOR'S LIE (Book #2)
CUL DE SAC (Book #3)
SILENT NEIGHBOR (Book #4)
HOMECOMING (Book #5)
TINTED WINDOWS (Book #6)

KATE WISE MYSTERY SERIES

IF SHE KNEW (Book #1)
IF SHE SAW (Book #2)
IF SHE RAN (Book #3)
IF SHE HID (Book #4)
IF SHE FLED (Book #5)
IF SHE FEARED (Book #6)
IF SHE HEARD (Book #7)

THE MAKING OF RILEY PAIGE SERIES
WATCHING (Book #1)
WAITING (Book #2)
LURING (Book #3)
TAKING (Book #4)
STALKING (Book #5)
KILLING (Book #6)

RILEY PAIGE MYSTERY SERIES
ONCE GONE (Book #1)
ONCE TAKEN (Book #2)
ONCE CRAVED (Book #3)
ONCE LURED (Book #4)
ONCE HUNTED (Book #5)
ONCE PINED (Book #6)
ONCE FORSAKEN (Book #7)
ONCE COLD (Book #8)
ONCE STALKED (Book #9)
ONCE LOST (Book #10)
ONCE BURIED (Book #11)
ONCE BOUND (Book #12)
ONCE TRAPPED (Book #13)
ONCE DORMANT (Book #14)
ONCE SHUNNED (Book #15)
ONCE MISSED (Book #16)
ONCE CHOSEN (Book #17)

MACKENZIE WHITE MYSTERY SERIES
BEFORE HE KILLS (Book #1)
BEFORE HE SEES (Book #2)
BEFORE HE COVETS (Book #3)
BEFORE HE TAKES (Book #4)

BEFORE HE NEEDS (Book #5)
BEFORE HE FEELS (Book #6)
BEFORE HE SINS (Book #7)
BEFORE HE HUNTS (Book #8)
BEFORE HE PREYS (Book #9)
BEFORE HE LONGS (Book #10)
BEFORE HE LAPSES (Book #11)
BEFORE HE ENVIES (Book #12)
BEFORE HE STALKS (Book #13)
BEFORE HE HARMS (Book #14)

AVERY BLACK MYSTERY SERIES
CAUSE TO KILL (Book #1)
CAUSE TO RUN (Book #2)
CAUSE TO HIDE (Book #3)
CAUSE TO FEAR (Book #4)
CAUSE TO SAVE (Book #5)
CAUSE TO DREAD (Book #6)

KERI LOCKE MYSTERY SERIES
A TRACE OF DEATH (Book #1)
A TRACE OF MURDER (Book #2)
A TRACE OF VICE (Book #3)
A TRACE OF CRIME (Book #4)
A TRACE OF HOPE (Book #5)

Lightning Source UK Ltd.
Milton Keynes UK
UKHW010254090223
416650UK00002B/391